Corgi Capers:
Deceit on Dorset Drive

Val Muller

Corgi Capers: Deceit on Dorset Drive

Corgi Capers: Deceit on Dorset Drive

Publishers Note:

This is a work of fiction. All names, charac-ters, places, and events are the work of the author's imagination. Any resemblance to real persons, places, or events is coincidental.

Cover Art: Justin James

Corgi Capers: Deceit on Dorset Drive

Corgi Capers: Deceit on Dorset Drive

Corgi Capers: Deceit on Dorset Drive

Corgi Capers: Deceit on Dorset Drive

Dedication

To my grandfather, who I met in a dream,
For pushing me to be what I otherwise only
might have been.

Acknowledgments

To my first readers, Michelle Muller and Eric
Egger — for the comments, suggestions, and
patience through the drafts. To my second
readers, Kathryn Ives and Allen Egger — for
the feedback and encouragement. To my final
draft readers, Madison McKay — for being my
first test-reader; and my sister Lisa Muller —
for only reading when you're angry. To my
parents, Michelle and Walter — for your un-
ending encouragement and belief in me. To
"CB" — for keeping it real. To Voula of Voula
Trip Photography — for the pictures and pro-
fessionalism. To Judy Roth — for the keen
eye. To Marie McGaha at DWB, without whom
this book would not be in your hands.
And to Yoda and Leia—Woof!

Corgi Capers: Deceit on Dorset Drive

Corgi Capers: Deceit on Dorset Drive

PROLOGUE
A Princess' Premonition

In the little Pennsylvania town of Stoney Brook, at the end of a rocky road, was a place where the crickets chirped just a little louder. A place where the summer grass smelled just a little sweeter. A place called Pickwick Farm. Pickwick Farm was home to two people, twelve chickens, two goats, three sheep, a horse, and six dogs.

Six corgis, to be exact.

On this cool August morning, one of the dogs, Owl, was already awake. He patrolled the farm faithfully by the side of his favorite Person, Farmer Pickwick.

"We've got to make sure the farm is in order," Farmer Pickwick told Owl. "We'll have some special visitors today."

Owl barked twice and twirled around in the dewy grass.

Inside the small farmhouse, four sleeping puppies and their mother heard Owl's excited barks. They yelped and jumped up all at once. Their warm comforter became a tangle of paws and ears.

Sparkles, their mother, stretched and turned over. "Go back to sleep, puppies," she yawned.

The largest puppy plopped down next to her, cuddling on the comforter. "Good boy, One," Sparkles said. One, the first to be born, was the largest and most obedient puppy.

Two, the second to be born, stretched out next to his brother. Sparkles nuzzled them while she kept an eye on the other puppies scuffling near the kitchen sink.

"Three and Four," Sparkles called. "Back to sleep!"

Four, the smallest of the puppies and the only female, was tugging on one of Three's tall ears. She wagged her tail and bit down hard. Three yelped and skittered back to the comforter to cuddle next to his brothers. Four's ears darted back, and she ran in frustrated circles near the stove.

"I want to play, play, *play*!" she yelped.

But Sparkles and the other puppies ignored Four. Before long she sulked back to the comforter to talk to her favorite brother.

"Three, Three, *Three*!" she cried.

"Go back to sleep," Three said.

"I can't."

Three fought drooping eyelids. "Why?"

"I have a feeling about today."

"What kind of feeling?"

"Like something special's going to happen. And I dreamed a strange word."

Three's eyes popped open. "What word?" he asked, his tail wagging.

"*Princess*," Four said. "What does it mean?"

Three wanted very much to discuss Four's new word, but he had to be quiet: footsteps echoed on the stairs.

Corgi Capers: Deceit on Dorset Drive

"Shhhh," Sparkles whispered. "Here come our People."

"I *said* the word was *princess*," Four pouted. "What does it mean? Tell me, tell me, *tell me!*"

But before Three could answer, Grandma Pickwick appeared at the kitchen door. The puppies ran over to greet her, their tails wagging and their ears pressed happily back against their heads. And in the excitement, even Four forgot all about her strange new word.

~ ONE ~
A Lucky Break

Adam Hollinger was the last boy left at practice. Again. Patrick, Coach Harris' son, sat next to him in the shade under the bleachers. The two were covered in dust from the field. A clay-red skid mark stained Patrick's pants from his slide into third. The boys' Lancaster Reds baseball hats were lined with sweat from the morning's practice. While Coach Harris spoke on his cell phone, the boys read the newest edition of *The Adventures of Logan Zephyr and the Stellar Squadron*. This volume was titled *Logan and the Sapphire Kingdom*.

"This is the coolest part," Patrick said, turning the page. He had already read the comic five times. He practically knew it by heart.

"Why?" Adam asked.

"It's where Logan Zephyr finds a space dog."

"A space dog? Cool!" Adam smiled, looking at the green puppy with three tails and two antennas.

"Wouldn't it be cool to have a space dog as a pet?" Patrick asked.

"It'd be cool to have *any* dog," Adam sighed. "My parents have been promising me a dog for over a year now."

"Why don't you get one, then?"

Corgi Capers: Deceit on Dorset Drive

"Dad doesn't really want one. He's always busy with his architecture business. Mom says it's hard for him to be working for himself. He's always either in his office or meeting with clients. Every time I mention a dog, Dad changes the subject. Besides, my parents don't think Courtney's responsible enough."

Patrick laughed. "I don't think your sister's responsible enough, either!"

Patrick had known Adam long enough to see Courtney's bad attitude worsen since she started middle school.

"I think my mom would like a dog, though," Adam said. "She had one when she was a kid. If we could only convince Dad..."

"Speaking of your mom," Patrick said. "Where do you think she is?"

Adam shrugged. "I don't think she's ever been on time."

A tall shadow blocked the sunlight, and the boys looked up to see Coach Harris standing over them. He had finished his phone conversation.

"Well, boys." He sounded disappointed. "That was Bryce's mother. I found out why Bryce wasn't at practice today."

"What happened, Dad?" Patrick asked.

"Last night Bryce was skateboarding. He fell and broke his wrist. His doctor told him he won't be able to pitch for the rest of the season."

"He's going to miss Autumn League?" Adam asked.

Corgi Capers: Deceit on Dorset Drive

Autumn League was the post-season travel league made up of the best players in each region. The biggest honor for players Adam's age was to be selected for the all-star team.

Coach Harris sighed.

"He was our secret weapon," Patrick sighed. "He could strike out *anyone!*"

"Our games start in just a week," Adam added. "What'll we do?"

"The only thing we can do. We'll find someone else on the team who can pitch." Coach got a little sparkle in his eye. "While we're here waiting, let's give your arm a try, Adam."

Adam's ears turned bright red, something they did when he was embarrassed or nervous. "Me? Pitch?" He was an outfielder. He'd always been an outfielder.

"Sure, why not?" Coach insisted. He was halfway to the field, catcher's mitt already on his hand.

Adam shuffled out from under the bleachers. He pulled on his red cap and gave Patrick his comic book. "I guess I'll have to finish reading this later."

"You can borrow it," said Patrick. "I'd give just about anything — even my limited edition Logan Zephyr comic — to see you try to pitch!"

Corgi Capers: Deceit on Dorset Drive

~ TWO ~
Sparkle's Pride

In the kitchen at Pickwick Farm, Grandma Pickwick set out a large bowl of kibble for Sparkles and the puppies to share. Sparkles ate slowly, watching her puppies through the corner of her eye. One, Two, and Three ate hungrily. But each time Four approached, the puppies growled at her, sending her away from the food.

"Why won't you let me eat?" Four protested.

"Because you bite my ears all the time," Three explained.

"And you bark in my face," added Two.

"And you don't listen to Ma," said One.

"Hmph," Four pouted. "Ma, no one will let me eat."

Sparkles finished chewing and turned to little Four. "What they say is true, Four. You're always picking on your brothers. And you rarely listen to me. Maybe it's time you start being a good girl."

"But I'm hungry, hungry, *hungry*!" Four squealed, jumping on each of her brothers despite their growls.

"Maybe you should apologize to them," Sparkles suggested.

"Never!" Four barked and barked and ran around the kitchen in circles. Before long, she was out of breath. "I'm hungry," she panted, plopping down next to her mother. Still, her brothers wouldn't let her have any of the food.

"I still think you should try apologizing," Sparkles said.

"Fine. I'm sorry, One. I'm sorry, Two."

Her brothers looked at her skeptically.

"I really am," Four insisted, rolling onto her back.

One and Two stepped out of the way, allowing her to eat some of the kibble.

"What about me?" Three asked. "Are you sorry you bite my ears all the time?"

Four laughed. "Not at all. You're my favorite brother, and biting your ears is what I love best!"

When they finished eating, Sparkles called her puppies back to the comforter. One and Two sat together, nudging each other playfully. Three sat and dropped his head to stare at the floor. He sensed something serious in the way his mother waited.

"Where's Four?" Sparkles asked.

"Chasing a mouse in the pantry," One answered.

"She's in trouble now," Two whispered.

Sparkles barked loudly. A moment later, a tiny mouse scurried across the floor, and Four came skittering behind it. The mouse disappeared into a hole in the wall, and Four slid into place between Two and Three, knocking them out of her way with a mischievous gleam in her eye.

Corgi Capers: Deceit on Dorset Drive

"I used to be as wild as you," Sparkles told Four. "But it got me into trouble in those days. One time I chased a rabbit all the way across the farm. My People shouted for me to stop, but I wouldn't listen. I ran until I fell into the stream. The water was so cold I almost drowned. Thank goodness Farmer Pickwick saved me."

Her eyes sparkled. "Another time, I got so excited eating some peanut butter out of Grandma Pickwick's hand that I nipped her finger. She got so mad she smacked me with a rolled-up newspaper. It hurt my feelings more than it hurt my behind, but you puppies have to control yourselves when you get too excited." She looked into each of her puppies' eyes. "I remember when you four were just little balls of fur..."

"Why is she telling us all this?" Two whispered.

"I don't know," Four said. "But I'd sure like to know what *peanut butter* is!"

"Today is a very special day," Sparkles continued. "Grandma Pickwick is about to take you all outside. When you get there I want you on your best behavior. If you don't behave, you won't get chosen by your People."

"Won't you be watching?" Three asked.

"Not this time, Three." She gave him a loving kiss on the muzzle. "My time to watch you has passed. You're moving on to a new time in your lives."

Corgi Capers: Deceit on Dorset Drive

Three whined.

"Don't be scared. You'll all find wonderful homes, and wonderful People. I overheard Grandma Pickwick talking to Grandpa. There's a Person out there for each of you, a Person destined to find you — just like how Grandpa and Grandma Pickwick found me. I had been lost in the pumpkin patch one cold evening when they found me, and as soon as I saw them, I knew they were mine..."

"You mean we won't be living here forever with you?" Three asked.

But Sparkles couldn't answer, for Grandma Pickwick's footsteps were getting closer.

"I love you all, my puppies," Sparkles said. "Now go out and live — and above all be happy!"

Grandma Pickwick entered the kitchen with a large cardboard box. She pet Sparkles lovingly, then picked up each of the four puppies, placed them gently in the box, and started for the door. The puppies didn't understand why, but they felt a mix of sadness and excitement. As Grandma Pickwick carried them away, all four sets of big, watery eyes turned toward Sparkles.

Just as the puppies were carried out of sight, Sparkles gave one loving bark before curling up on the blanket that still smelled like her puppies for some much-needed rest.

~ THREE ~
The Trouble with GPS

On Dorset Drive, exactly 25.7 miles from Pickwick Farm, Mrs. Hollinger raced down her driveway. She was late leaving to pick up Adam from baseball practice. No matter how early she tried to leave, something always made her late. This time, she had been editing the last pages of a client's novel and lost track of time.

But before Mrs. Hollinger could leave, Mrs. Pinkney rushed outside in tears. Mrs. Pinkney was the Hollingers' next-door neighbor, and she was usually calm and reserved. But not today.

"What's wrong?" Mrs. Hollinger asked, glancing quickly at her watch.

"I was at the denthist," Mrs. Pinkney said.

"The *what*?" Mrs. Hollinger asked.

"The denthist," Mrs. Pinkney said, pointing to her mouth. "I had to get a tooth drilthed."

Mrs. Hollinger nodded. "I guess the Novocain hasn't worn off yet?"

Mrs. Pinkney shook her head. "But when I goth home, the back window was broken, and all my sthuff was gone!"

"Gone?"

Mrs. Pinkney nodded. "I was justh on the phone with the insuranth — insurance —

company."

"It must be that serial burglar," Mrs. Hollinger gasped. "The police haven't caught him yet."

Mrs. Pinkney sobbed. "My jewelry box is empty, and it had my grandmother's wedding ring in it. It wasn't worth much, but it's been in the family for years. I was going to give it to my granddaughter one day." Mrs. Pinkney sniffled into a tissue.

"That's terrible," Mrs. Hollinger said.

"It was white gold with embellishments that looked like swirling waves of the ocean, and six amethysts set in the waves. My grandmother met my grandfather at the beach..."

"It sounds beautiful," Mrs. Hollinger said, looking at her watch again.

"It was. And on the inside, it was engraved: *the ocean eternal, like our love.*"

Mrs. Hollinger placed a hand on Mrs. Pinkney's arm. "Such a shame that someone would take something so sentimental."

This started a new round of sniffling. "All the windows were closed and locked," Mrs. Pinkney insisted. "All the doors were bolted, but someone smashed through the back window anyway."

A moment later, a police car pulled into the Pinkney's driveway. "I'm sorry, Eden," Mrs. Hollinger said. "I'll catch up with you after the police have left."

Mrs. Pinkney sniffed into the tissue as

she watched Mrs. Hollinger rush into her
minivan and drive down the street.
~ * ~
Mrs. Hollinger tried to hurry to the
baseball field, but none of the traffic lights
were green. At the first red light, she tapped
her hand impatiently on the steering wheel
and squinted at a sign on the side of the road.
It read:
TAG SALE
SATURDAY
8 A.M. THRU 3 P.M.
"Thru?" she asked herself. "That sign is
spelled wrong! It should read T-H-R-O-U-G-H."
Behind her, a line of cars beeped. The
light had turned green but she was too distracted to notice.
"Do I turn right here, or left?" she
asked herself before deciding to go straight.
She often got lost. Adam and Courtney, and
even Mr. Hollinger, teased her about it.
"I'd better turn on my GPS," she told
herself.
At the next red light, she tried to turn
on her GPS navigation system, but the screen
stayed black.
"Not now," Mrs. Hollinger said. She
pushed the on/off button but nothing happened. She checked to make sure the GPS was
plugged in. It was. She couldn't find anything
that was causing it not to work: it was just
plain broken.
Before long, traffic started moving

again. Mrs. Hollinger looked at the blank GPS screen.

"Now which way do I turn at this next intersection?" she asked herself. "Is it left or right?"

~ * ~

When she finally arrived at the baseball field, she was surprised to see Adam pitching to Patrick with Coach Harris watching.

"Good arm, Adam!" Coach said, as Mrs. Hollinger approached the field.

"Sorry I'm late," she apologized. "How was practice?"

"Practice went good." Coach Harris gave the thumbs up.

Mrs. Hollinger cringed. "You mean practice went *well*?" she whispered.

Mrs. Hollinger was a professional copy-editor, and it was her job to catch grammatical mistakes. Bad grammar was her pet peeve.

But Coach Harris was too busy talking to notice.

"Bring it in, boys!" he yelled and turned back to Mrs. Hollinger. "Looks like it'll be a great post-season. Except for one thing. Our pitcher broke his wrist last night. He's out for the season."

Coach Harris looked at Adam and chomped on his gum for a moment. "Adam's pretty good at pitching."

"Is he?" Mrs. Hollinger asked.

"He did pretty good."

Corgi Capers: Deceit on Dorset Drive

"Pretty *well*," she corrected.

"Yes. Encourage Adam to keep practic-ing." Coach Harris gave Adam a firm pat on the back. "I guess I'll have to call the rest of the team and let them know about Bryce. I'll give everyone a day or two to practice, and then I'll hold try-outs for pitcher."

"Next practice?" Patrick asked.

"We've got to have a pitcher soon. Our games begin right after school starts."

"Well," Mrs. Hollinger said. "I'm sure Adam would love to try out. Wouldn't you, Adam?"

Adam's ears turned red. "Next practice is only two days away."

"That don't matter."

Mrs. Hollinger scrunched her nose at the coach's grammar.

"I guess I could try out." Adam still looked uncertain.

"Good," said Coach. "I got a feeling about you."

Adam smiled.

"Don't forget this," Patrick said. He handed Adam the Logan Zephyr comic book. "Try to finish it by next practice. I can't wait to talk about Logan's newest adventure!"

"Sure. And thanks." Adam waved and climbed into the back of the minivan.

"Just be careful," Patrick called through the window. "That comic book's a limited edition!"

Corgi Capers: Deceit on Dorset Drive

Adam nodded as Mrs. Hollinger climbed into the driver's seat.

"Were you waiting long?" she asked, starting the engine.

Adam shrugged. After nine years, he'd gotten used to his mother's tardiness. "I got to practice pitching. Besides, it gave me time to catch up on my reading."

He leaned into the front seat and held out the comic book for his mom to see. "This time Logan Zephyr and his crew get stuck on a planet made of quicksand."

He opened the comic book to show her. "And he even found this space dog that has three tails and two anten..."

"That's nice, Adam," Mrs. Hollinger said. "But we've got to hurry to the mall to pick up Courtney."

"Stupid Courtney," Adam muttered as he shuffled his way to the very back seat of the minivan.

"Actually Adam, I need you to sit up front with me."

"Up front? Why? Courtney always gets to sit up front."

Ever since she entered middle school, Courtney had been bossing everyone around — even Mr. and Mrs. Hollinger. Now that she was going to be a seventh grader, her attitude was much worse.

"The GPS broke," Mrs. Hollinger said sheepishly. "So I need you to help me find my way to the mall."

Corgi Capers: Deceit on Dorset Drive

"Oh, Mom." Adam placed Patrick's comic book carefully in the magazine holder behind the seat and moved up to the front. With Mrs. Hollinger's sense of direction, it was going to be a long afternoon.

~ FOUR ~
Not Just a Dream

The August morning had warmed, and Grandma Pickwick brought the four corgi puppies to a large pen in front of the farmhouse. She then busied herself with a flat piece of wood.

The puppies amused themselves by jumping in the air to chase dragonflies. Four was the best jumper. She almost caught a dragonfly, but it changed course at the last second and she fell to the ground, landing on Two. Two rolled out from under her and took a good long stretch.

"What's she doing?" Two asked, motioning with his nose to Grandma Pickwick. "It smells kinda funny."

"I don't know," Four said as she scratched her ear. "Maybe it has to do with that feeling I had this morning."

"Stop worrying and chase these dragonflies!" yelled One. He jumped in the air, snapping at a dragonfly that was a bit too high.

"Hmmm." Three paused, quietly contemplating the situation. "It seems she's painting something."

"Painting? What's that?" asked Four.

"Is it good to eat?" One asked, trying to jump out of the pen. "I'll bet it tastes great." He barked enthusiastically.

Corgi Capers: Deceit on Dorset Drive

"No," Three explained calmly. "Paint is not good to eat. And I don't quite know what she's painting."

"I had a dream early this morning," Two said. "In my dream, a little boy came here and picked me up and took me to his home. He was so nice to me, and when we got to his house, he had a little bed set up for me, and some chew toys, and a water dish, and a food bowl, and…"

Two plopped onto the ground, resting his head on his front paws and looking up at the sky with big, sad eyes.

"Whoa, Two," One said. "Getting a little carried away, aren't you? It was only a dream."

"I know," Two said. "But I wish it could last forever."

With that, Grandma Pickwick held up the sign she'd been painting. She called to Farmer Pickwick, who was seated on the front porch. "How does it look, Grandpa? Can you read it from there?"

The old man squinted in the sun. "Looks good," he said.

Though he was the smartest of the puppies, Three still didn't know how to read the language of People. So when Grandma Pickwick held up what she had written, he had no idea what it said. But Three howled softly and soon the other puppies joined in, whining and yelping and jumping against the side of the pen.

Grandpa Pickwick laughed. "Do you hear that, Grandma? I think they want to know what it says." He approached their pen and patted each of them on the head. "That sign's gonna get you all new homes. You know what it says, pups?"

All four barked.

"It says 'Corgi Puppies for Sale.'"

Puppies One, Two, and Four wagged their tails at Grandpa. But Puppy Three was too busy studying the letters, his head cocked as he tried to memorize the first four words of his written People vocabulary.

Corgi Capers: Deceit on Dorset Drive

~ FIVE ~
Sibling Rivalry

During weekends and summers, Courtney spent nearly every waking moment at
Park City Mall. Usually she got a ride home
with Aileen's mother, but today Mrs. Hollinger
agreed to pick her up.

"I can't believe we're going to the mall
without the GPS," Adam groaned. "We'll never get there. You shoulda had Courtney get a
ride home with her friends."

"Should *have*," Mrs. Hollinger corrected. "It's 'should *have*.' And yes, I should
have!"

"That's okay. You can leave Courtney
there as long as you want. I'm sure she
wouldn't mind. She'd live at the mall if she
could. She's the biggest shopaholic I ever
seen."

"I ever *saw*," Mrs. Hollinger corrected
again. "That reminds me. Grab my cell phone.
We should tell Courtney we'll be late."

Adam looked skeptically at his mother.
Courtney and Adam were so used to Mrs. Hollinger being late they expected it. In fact, the
only surprise would be if she were actually on
time. Besides, since their big argument this
morning, Adam and his sister weren't exactly
on speaking terms.

"I don't want to call her."

"I can't call while I'm driving. It's dan-

Corgi Capers: Deceit on Dorset Drive

gerous. Besides, I'm trying not to get lost."
Mrs. Hollinger snickered and pointed out the
window. "Look at that billboard. It really
needs a comma between 'buy' and 'save.'"

Adam rolled his eyes and dialed his sister's number.

Courtney answered on the first ring.
Without saying hello, she said, "I knew you'd
be late, Mom, so we're still at Maxi's trying
on dresses. I found this awesome blue one
with sequin straps and…"

Adam huffed. Lately all his sister
thought about was herself. "How about a 'hello' first, Courtney?"

"Eww, it's *you*. I'm surprised Mom let
you put your grubby little paws on her cell
phone."

"Maybe it's because I vacuumed the
minivan this morning even though it was your
turn. And even though it tired me out before
practice."

"Like you really need energy to stand
in the outfield all day, you little nerd. I probably got more exercise at the mall than you
did at practice. You're nothing but an outfielder."

Adam rolled his eyes. "I wasn't just in
the outfield today. I was pitching. Coach
wants me to try out for pitcher."

"A little nerd like you would never
make pitcher." Courtney's voice oozed with
attitude. In the background, Adam heard
Courtney's friends laughing.

"I'm not a nerd."

"Yes, you are."

"Am not."

"Are too."

Adam heard Aileen yell something in the background. She was Courtney's best friend and enjoyed teasing Adam almost as much as Courtney did. Courtney laughed, then repeated what Aileen had said. "You're a red-head, freckle-faced nerd!"

"Am not. Besides, you should have vac-uumed the van. It was your turn."

"Was not."

"Yes, it was."

"Was not."

"Was too."

"Kids," Mrs. Hollinger cried. "Enough!"

Courtney whispered into the phone, "Besides, I couldn't ruin my new manicure by running the vacuum cleaner. That's why I made you do it."

"So it *was* your turn. You admit it. You're such a —"

Mrs. Hollinger cleared her throat.

Adam didn't want to distract his mom from driving, so he changed the subject.

"Mom wanted me to let you know we'll be late. Her GPS broke."

"Maybe you'll never get here," Court-ney joked. "You'll end up in Hawaii!"

The siblings forgot their argument long enough to share a laugh.

Still snickering, Adam looked up and

saw a sign go by that read, *Park City Mall, Exit Here.*

"Mom, that was your exit!" But it was too late. Mrs. Hollinger had already passed it. "Looks like we'll have to turn around. This may take a while," Adam told his sister before hanging up.

"Hey, look at that truck." Mrs. Hollinger pointed at a soda truck. "Its slogan is missing a period at the end of the sentence!"

~ SIX ~
A Dream Comes True

Four barked from her pen as she watched Grandpa Pickwick return down the long gravel driveway.

"I put the sign up right along the road," he told Grandma.

Grandma was bent over the puppies trying to comb out their fluffy fur before any People came to look at them. Two, who she was combing — or trying to comb — was being more fidgety than usual. He kept trying to jump out of the pen.

"What's gotten into you, little pup?" Grandma asked. She bent down to calm the puppy.

Just then, the Pickwicks heard tires moving slowly along the gravel. From somewhere behind the farm house, Owl charged. As the car parked, he ran up to the window, howling at the driver.

A woman rolled down the window and peered out from the driver's seat. "My, he's alert," she said.

Grandpa walked over to pat Owl on the head. "Name's Owl. We called him that because his howl reminds us of the way an owl hoots." Grandpa noticed the hesitant look in the woman's eyes. "He's alert, but friendly."

"Oh." The woman got out of the car,

Corgi Capers: Deceit on Dorset Drive

and in a moment Owl's stubby tail was wagging so hard that his entire body wiggled.

"We were driving along and saw that sign out there. Corgi puppies for sale. I promised Connor I'd get him a puppy for his birthday. Connor's my son," she explained. She opened the back door of the car, and a young boy stepped out.

"Grandma," Grandpa called. "Someone saw your sign."

Grandma put down the fidgeting Two and walked toward the woman and her son.

While Grandma was absorbed in conversation, Two couldn't stay still.

"Two, get a hold of yourself," One said.

Two tried to stop jumping. "The boy," he yelped, not even bothering to keep his voice down. "That's the boy from my dream. It's him!"

The other puppies tried, but none could calm Two. Before long, Owl approached.

"Two," Owl whispered. "Calm down. If you look *too* wild, you'll never get chosen." He turned to the rest of the puppies. "Puppies, this little boy belongs to Two. You let him get chosen."

The puppies nodded. Owl nudged Two through the pen and howled quietly as he ran to the front porch.

Before long, Grandma, Grandpa, Con-

Corgi Capers: Deceit on Dorset Drive

nor, and his mother approached the pen of puppies. The four dogs sat watching. Connor stared back, lips stretched in a wide smile. All of the puppies had short legs and long bodies, and their large ears already stuck straight into the air. Tricolor, they were a mix of white, black, and tan. They all had white paws that looked like socks, white collars and underbellies, and black overcoats and stubby black tails. Tan markings ran along their legs, the tops of their heads, and their ears. Each muzzle was covered in a white triangle, each triangle slightly different in size or shape.

"Which one do you want, Connor?" the woman asked.

Connor shrugged. "I don't know."

Four ran up to the boy, wagging her stubby tail and whimpering.

"This one's cute," said Connor.

From the porch, Owl growled. Four cried and ran to the back of the pen.

"Maybe that's not the one for you," Connor's mom said. "Maybe you want one a little less wild."

Owl barked. Three and One stepped aside, leaving Two staring at the boy.

"This puppy!" Connor insisted, looking at Two. Two stuck his nose through the pen, kissing Connor gently on the hand. Connor giggled.

"He looks very happy," Three said.

"Which one?" Four asked. "The boy, or Two?"

"Both," Three answered.

~ SEVEN ~
Are We There Yet?

When Mrs. Hollinger finally found the mall, Courtney was waiting outside surrounded by three huge shopping bags. With her head down in concentration, her fingers flew across the keypad of her cell phone. She didn't even stop texting when her mother's minivan pulled up.

Mrs. Hollinger rolled down the window. "Did your friends leave already?"

Courtney finished sending her text message before answering, "No, they're sitting in Mrs. Ellison's car." She pointed to a parking spot nearby. "I was just texting Aileen now."

Mrs. Hollinger waved to Mrs. Ellison, who waved back. Aileen waved as well.

Marnie Ellison, Aileen's younger sister, stuck her tongue out at Adam through the window as Mrs. Ellison drove off. Adam's ears turned bright red. He hoped Marnie didn't notice.

Courtney laughed and put her bags in the back of the minivan, then turned to Adam in the front seat.

"Get in the back," she whispered. "I get to sit up front."

Adam looked at Mrs. Hollinger, but she was too busy fidgeting with the broken GPS.

"Do it, or I'll tell the whole school you have a crush on Ms. Wilkerson." Courtney flashed a toothy grin and snapped her bubble gum.

Ms. Wilkerson had been Adam's fourth-grade science teacher last year. In science class, Adam always knew the answers, and he often volunteered to help pass out papers. Many of his classmates accused him of being a teacher's pet — especially Marnie Ellison.

What's worse, Marnie told her sister Aileen about anything that could possibly embarrass Adam. And of course, Aileen gossiped it to Courtney, who was always looking for new ways to torment her brother. It was Marnie who suggested starting a rumor that Adam had a crush on Ms. Wilkerson. That was all Adam needed — to start fifth grade with the whole school thinking he had a crush on the science teacher!

"But I *don't* have a crush on her," Adam protested.

Courtney snickered. "I'm a seventh grader. Your classmates will believe anything I tell them."

"Fine." Adam climbed into the back. "But that means you have to help Mom navigate."

"Whatever." Courtney slouched in the front seat. Almost immediately, she flipped open her cell phone and started texting.

Adam climbed over the huge shopping bags to sit in the very back row — as far away from Courtney as possible.

Corgi Capers: Deceit on Dorset Drive

"Geez, do you have any money left?"

"Nope. I spent every cent of my baby-sitting earnings. I even had to borrow money from Aileen to buy an ice cream."

Adam rolled his eyes. He had been mowing lawns the entire summer, and he already had nearly three hundred dollars in his savings account. He was saving for something big — though he wasn't sure what yet.

"Don't you have enough stuff, Courtney?" he asked. "Save some money for a rainy day."

"Whatever, Nerd. You wouldn't understand. It's different in middle school. We're not all bookworms, like you. We don't sit around reading comic books — or doing homework."

"Caring about school doesn't make me a nerd." Adam crossed his arms and stared out the window. "And I'm playing Autumn League. Only the best players in Pennsylvania get to play Autumn League. Besides, nerds don't play baseball!"

"There's a first for everything," Courtney snapped.

As they left the mall parking lot, Adam noticed all the light posts were decorated with large, light-up red roses.

"Hey," he said. "Red roses. Like the Lancaster Reds."

He smiled at the sound of his team's name. Taking off his baseball hat, he looked at the logo: a red and white baseball decorated with a small red rose.

"I think it's a stupid name," Courtney said. "I don't like the color red, anyway. They should have picked something cooler, like purple."

"Courtney," Mrs. Hollinger scolded. "Try to be nice. Besides, there's a history behind his team's name."

"Yeah, Courtney," Adam said. "We're from Lancaster. Even you should know that Lancaster's emblem is the red rose."

"Whatever, Nerd." She rolled her eyes and turned back to her texting.

As Mrs. Hollinger drove onto the highway entrance ramp, she and Adam let out a collective sigh: the highway toward home was jammed with bumper-to-bumper traffic. The vehicles lined up like cars in a never-ending train, and the heat reflecting off the pavement made the air look wavy and nightmarish.

The afternoon sun reflected off the side-view mirrors in blinding spots of light. Adam squinted.

"At this rate, it'll take forever to get home." Mrs. Hollinger groaned. "Thank goodness we have air conditioning."

"Still, I don't want to be stuck in the car with *her* any longer than I have to," Adam said.

Courtney was too busy texting to reply.

Mrs. Hollinger took a deep breath. "Well, I guess while we're stuck here, I might

Corgi Capers: Deceit on Dorset Drive

as well tell you about poor Mrs. Pinkney. Courtney, put away your cell phone."

Adam froze. "What's wrong, Mom?"

"Mrs. Pinkney's house was broken into this morning."

"The Pinkneys' house," Adam said. "But that's right next door!"

"Was it the same burglar?" Courtney asked.

"The police had just arrived as I was leaving, so I don't know yet. But probably it's the same one who's been burglarizing other homes in our neighborhood."

"The serial burglar," Adam whispered.

The car grew quiet.

"Maybe we should take the Pinkneys some dinner," Adam said finally.

"That's a good idea. I'll cook some extra portions tonight."

The car quieted again. The news about their neighbors had dampened everyone's spirits. To make matters worse, the car had barely moved since entering the highway.

"We should get home," Courtney said. "To make sure *our* house is okay."

"Do you know a back way, Mom?" Adam asked.

"*I* do." Courtney grinned confidently. "If you get off at the next exit, I'll show you how to get home, Mom."

Mrs. Hollinger looked skeptical. "Maybe it's best to stay on the highway. Even with traffic, at least we won't get lost."

"Trust me, Mom," Courtney insisted. "Aileen's dad took us the back way last time we went to the mall. I know it. Trust me."

"Well..." Mrs. Hollinger looked out at the highway. Traffic still hadn't moved an inch. Car horns beeped constantly. On the side of the road, a family was having a fast-food picnic on the trunk of their car.

"If we stay here, we won't get home 'til dinnertime," Adam said.

"You should know," Courtney said with an attitude. "You're such a nerd — you can probably calculate how long it will take. Probably without a calculator, too. It's like one of those horrible word problems: A car leaves the mall at two thirty-five traveling at a speed of..."

Courtney's cell phone beeped with a new message, which distracted her enough to stop teasing Adam.

"I hate being stuck in here with Courtney," Adam mumbled.

He tried to ignore his sister, but he hated being called a nerd. He remembered all the things he'd been called in the past year at school: nerd, dork, bookworm, teacher's pet, goody-goody, red-head, and freckle-face. He frowned. He liked to think of himself as good at other things besides school, like baseball, camping, reading. But everyone only seemed to see him as a nerd.

Especially Marnie Ellison.

Adam stared out the window in frustra-

Corgi Capers: Deceit on Dorset Drive

tion until he remembered he had borrowed Patrick's comic book. He gently took it from the magazine holder — careful not to bend any corners — and began reading from the beginning.

"Alright," Mrs. Hollinger said finally. "I'll get off at the next exit. But Courtney, you've got to help me navigate. I've never gone this way before."

"Yeah, Mom. Once you get off the exit, just drive straight until I tell you to turn," Courtney said — only half listening — as she began typing another text to her friend.

~ EIGHT ~
Owl's Request

Back on Pickwick Farm, three puppies remained in the pen.

"Where did Two go?" Four asked.

"He found a new home," Three explained.

"But when will he be back?"

"He won't," Three said, trying to remain patient. Four was easily excitable, and it was difficult for her to stay focused long enough to understand what was happening.

"Wait, where did Two go again?"

Three sighed and turned to One. "Did you hear what they named him?"

"Lion," One said.

"I thought his name was Two. Two, Two, *Two!*" Four shouted.

"No, Four," Owl said, coming over from the porch. He stood very close to her so that she backed down in submission. It helped to calm and focus her. "When you find your Person, he or she will give you a name."

"Why did they name him Lion?" Four asked. "His name is Two, Two, *Two!*" She dug at the ground in frustration.

"Didn't you see? Two wouldn't stop eating dandelions. So the boy decided to call him 'Lion' for short."

"A fitting name," Three agreed.

"But his name is Two," Four insisted.

Corgi Capers: Deceit on Dorset Drive

"And when's he coming back, anyway?"

One chewed playfully on Four's ear to distract her from whining. In the meantime, Owl took Three aside.

"Three," Owl said. "Four has a lot of energy. She's the runt of the litter, but she makes up for her size with wildness. She'll be a handful to her Person. Four has always liked you. Maybe it would be best if the two of you stick together. You could look out for her. Make sure she doesn't get into any trouble."

Three wagged his tail. "Yes, Pa," he agreed, proud that his father had such confidence in him.

Owl nuzzled his son. "That's a good boy," he whispered.

They turned to watch Four pulling up clumps of grass and running in wide circles. Three looked back at Owl and wondered just what he had gotten himself into.

Corgi Capers: Deceit on Dorset Drive

~ NINE ~
The Right Turn

After twenty minutes of traffic, Mrs. Hollinger pulled off at the very next exit.

"Finally," Courtney sighed as her mother accelerated down the exit ramp. "There's really bad cell reception back there."

Her fingers flew as she caught up on the messages she'd missed.

"Don't forget to tell me when to turn," Mrs. Hollinger reminded her daughter. "Remember, you're the only person in this car who's taken this way home before."

"Okay," Courtney said, briefly looking up. "Just keep going straight until I tell you. It's easy to get back. Aileen just texted me to say that her mom's taking the back way, too!"

"That's nice, dear. But remember to keep an eye on the road."

After a minute of pushing buttons, Courtney laughed.

"Marnie just told Aileen something funny about Adam."

Adam tensed in the back seat.

Courtney pulled down the sun visor and looked at him through the mirror.

"It turns out that the only reason Adam gets to try out for pitcher is because Bryce broke his arm. Marnie was at the skate park last night. She said Bryce was doing a trick

Corgi Capers: Deceit on Dorset Drive

move on a Rip Stick, and he fell at the last minute. There was even an ambulance.

"Too bad you never do anything cool like that, Adam. It figures the pitcher got injured. I knew you wouldn't get to try pitching unless you were the last resort."

Adam crossed his arms. Why was Marnie always so interested in making his life miserable? And Aileen was in seventh grade. Didn't she have anything better to do than help Courtney torment fifth graders?

Adam looked up front to see if his mother noticed Courtney's taunts. But as usual, she was distracted.

"Did you kids see that hand-made sign at the farm stand?" Mrs. Hollinger asked. "They spelled 'canteloupes' wrong! It should be c-a-n-t-a…"

Adam lost himself in Patrick's comic book. It was better than fighting with his sister or listening to his mother rant about spelling and grammar. He'd much rather read about the adventures of Logan Zephyr.

In this adventure, the Stellar Squadron landed on a planet made entirely of quicksand, and Logan's spaceship was sucked down below the surface. But just when they thought they were done for, they discovered something beneath the quicksand: a magnificent kingdom paved in sapphires.

Adam turned the page and tried to tune out his sister's beeping phone.

Corgi Capers: Deceit on Dorset Drive

Underneath the quicksand, Logan met Princess Sapphire. Her powers were strong enough to prevent the quicksand from seeping into the underground kingdom. She was beautiful and energetic, and her glowing blue sapphire palace was the most brilliant thing Logan Zephyr had ever seen.

The problem was that Princess Sapphire didn't get many visitors. She was so excited about having guests that she couldn't quite focus her attention on what Logan and his friends were saying — that they just wanted help getting home. Though Logan was mystified by the magical kingdom, he became annoyed at the energetic princess. She was too excited to help the crew get home.

Logan's heart belonged to outer space. He was an explorer eager to explore. But Princess Sapphire was the only one powerful enough to help the crew re-enter space. If she wanted, she could keep them captive forever.

In the last section of the comic book, the lonely princess decided that Logan and his crew should move to her planet — permanently. And being a princess, she always got what she wanted.

"So will you stay here with me?" Princess Sapphire asked Logan and his crew. Her eyes sparkled blue just like her sapphire castle. "Forever?"

Logan looked at his crew nervously. Sweat poured from his brow. He was about to answer the princess when —

Corgi Capers: Deceit on Dorset Drive

Just as Adam turned the page, Courtney whined, "Mom, you were supposed to turn
like a mile ago!"

"I was?"

"Yes!" Courtney said.

"Why didn't you tell me? You said you
knew how to get back. I told you I'd never
gone this way before."

Courtney's face blushed. "Sorry, I guess
I got caught up in texting."

"Sorry?" Adam said from the back seat.
"Did I just hear you say *sorry*? This is a first.
I'll have to mark the date on my calendar.
The day my sister actually apologized for
something. What a historical occasion!"

"Oh, be quiet, Adam. It's not like you
were helping. You're just sitting there reading
your stupid comic book." Courtney eyed Adam
through the sun visor's mirror.

"I'm reading about a character just like
you. She's unfocused and self-centered and
thinking about herself when she could be
helping everyone else."

"Yeah, well, I'd like to *be* her. She
doesn't have a stupid brother named Adam."

"Well you *are* like her. She's a princess, just like you. She's always thinking
about herself. She controls her kingdom and
gets away with whatever she wants. She always gets her way and never gets in trouble."

"Shut up, Adam. You ain't nothing but
a nerdy little — "

Corgi Capers: Deceit on Dorset Drive

"Courtney," Mrs. Hollinger scolded. Both Courtney and Adam looked up. "You know that 'ain't' isn't really a word. That's improper grammar!"

"Yeah, Courtney," Adam added. "A seventh grader should know better."

Mrs. Hollinger had already focused back on driving. To Courtney and Adam's horror, she decided to turn down a small and winding dirt road.

"Maybe there'll be someone here who can tell us how to get back," she said.

Adam and Courtney forgot their fighting and exchanged nervous glances. All they saw for miles was farmland. The road was so bumpy that they got thrown side-to-side in their seats, even with their seatbelts tightly fastened. Adam couldn't even finish reading his comic book.

Courtney looked at her cell phone. "Darn."

"What's that?" her mother asked.

"We must be in the middle of nowhere. I have *no* signal."

"Maybe if Courtney gets a signal on her phone we can just call Dad and ask him to look up directions for us."

"Dad's out meeting with clients all afternoon. He won't be back until later."

Adam sighed. His father was always busy with work.

"Here's something," Mrs. Hollinger said finally. It was a long, gravel road. A faded street sign read, "Pickwick Drive."

"Corgi puppies for sale?" Adam nearly jumped out of his seat at the sight of Grandma Pickwick's sign. "Mom, could we stop to look at them? You've been saying we could get a dog for like a year now!"

Even Courtney smiled and looked pleadingly at her mother.

Mrs. Hollinger studied the sign. "It's spelled correctly and everything," she said, as if that helped to convince her. "We'll stop, but only because I need directions."

"What about the puppies?" Adam asked.

"You can look. But that's all we're doing — just looking."

"Yeah," said Courtney. "Imagine how freaked out Dad would be if we came home with a puppy."

They pulled down the gravel drive, which was even bumpier than the main road. As they slowed to park, a full-grown corgi ran up to the car with sharp ears and stubby legs. He howled at them in his distinct manner that sounded strangely like an owl.

~ TEN ~
Three + Four = 2

"More people," barked One. "Maybe they're my People."

"I'm not sure," Three said.

Four couldn't help herself. She trembled with excitement, the hair on her back sticking straight up like a cat's. First she jumped up and down on her two back legs. With her ears sticking straight up and bouncing on just two legs, she looked like a baby kangaroo. When she tired of that, she still had lots of energy, so she grabbed a stick from the ground and ran around the pen wildly, growling and hopping over her two brothers every time she passed them, biting down on the stick to channel some of her energy.

"I guess *she'll* never get chosen, acting like that," One said.

"You're right," Three whispered.

Owl was at the minivan greeting the Hollingers. He especially seemed to like the boy and dropped to the ground, then rolled over, allowing Adam to rub his belly.

"He's a very good dog." Mrs. Hollinger smiled at Grandpa Pickwick. "I'm Susan Hollinger. These are my kids, Courtney and Adam."

"Pleased to meet you," Grandpa Pickwick said.

Corgi Capers: Deceit on Dorset Drive

"Are the puppies going to be like him?"
Adam asked. His eyes opened wide with excitement.

Grandpa Pickwick smiled. "They're all
different."

"They've all got their own personalities," Grandma Pickwick added. "Just like
people."

"And what's their mother like?" Mrs.
Hollinger asked.

"Oh, she's just as sweet as anything.
She's in the kitchen resting."

Courtney finally stepped out of the
minivan, her fingers still texting. She took a
look at Owl, who was still lying on his back,
having his belly rubbed by Adam. Then she
looked over at the pen and turned to Grandma
Pickwick in disgust.

"What's wrong with their legs? It's like
someone took the legs of a tiny dog and put
them on the body of a larger one. Or cut them
in half."

"Don't be rude," Mrs. Hollinger
warned, laughing in embarrassment.

"There's nothing wrong with them,"
Grandma Pickwick said patiently. "They're
Pembroke Welsh corgis. The corgi breed has
short legs, long bodies, and tall ears. It's what
makes them unique."

Courtney frowned. Her cell phone
beeped, and she pushed a button, reading her
newest message.

Corgi Capers: Deceit on Dorset Drive

"Aileen says she's never heard of corgis."

In the meantime, Owl rolled onto his side. He jumped up quickly, barked once at Adam, then ran to the front porch.

"Why don't you look at the puppies?" Mrs. Hollinger suggested. She looked Adam deep in the eye. "But remember, we're just looking."

"Okay, okay," Adam sighed, walking toward the pen. The gravel crunched under his feet. His heart beat in anticipation. He felt like Captain Logan Zephyr finding the space puppy.

"So you're interested in a puppy?" Grandpa Pickwick asked Mrs. Hollinger.

Mrs. Hollinger blushed. "No, actually."

Grandpa Pickwick frowned.

"I mean, maybe," Mrs. Hollinger said. "But that's not why we're here. I got lost coming from the highway. It's just a coincidence that we're here."

Grandpa Pickwick smiled, the wrinkles in his brow drawing his eyebrows upward.

"Oh, I've seen enough in my day to know a coincidence is often more than what it seems. I'll go write you directions back to the highway.

"In the meantime, why don't you go look at the puppies for yourself? They're already three months old, so you can see their personalities. And they're almost housebroken." He looked at Four. "Some of them, anyway."

At the puppies' pen, Mrs. Hollinger stared at Adam and Courtney. For the first time all day, they weren't fighting.

"That's incredible!" Mrs. Hollinger said. "Back in the car, they wouldn't stop arguing."

"Amazing how a little puppy can bring people together," Grandma Pickwick said with a wink.

Adam bent over the pen, holding out his arm. Immediately, One ran up to him, sniffed, then ran back to the middle of the pen.

"He doesn't smell like my Person ought to smell," he whispered to Three.

"That's because he isn't your person," Three answered. "He's mine."

With that, Three walked quietly to the boy. He sat down and stared straight into the boy's eyes, his tail wagging uncontrollably.

"This one's great," Adam yelled. He looked at his mom. He was sure there was a twinkle in her eye.

Grandma approached. "Yes, he's a great puppy. He's the only one without the fairy saddle."

"Fairy saddle?" Adam asked.

Grandma explained. "See, the corgis have what's called the 'fairy saddle.' It's a ring of white that goes from the top of their head down the back of their neck and wraps around their shoulders like a collar." She picked up One to demonstrate.

"Why's it called the fairy saddle?" Adam asked.

"If you look closely," Grandma explained, "it looks like the perfect-sized saddle for a fairy."

"Perfect*ly*-sized," Mrs. Hollinger muttered.

Grandma continued. "Legend has it that fairies back in the British Isles used corgis as transportation to do their mischievous errands, and the white markings are what was left behind of the fairies' saddle."

"Cool." Adam nodded.

"But this little pup," Grandma said, picking up Three, "doesn't have the fairy saddle. His marking starts at the top of his head, goes down the back of his neck, and then stops. And from what we've seen of his behavior so far, it's true to his personality. Of all the four puppies in the litter, this one is the least mischievous. He's never disobeyed us. He's always calm — unless he's scrapping with his sister."

"He sounds like you, Adam." Mrs. Hollinger laughed.

Grandma smiled. "He sure seems to like you," she said, handing the pup to Adam.

Three stayed very still, taking a deep whiff of the boy's scent. Adam looked down at the puppy, and the puppy looked back. Finally, Three gave Adam a kiss on the cheek.

Adam grinned from ear to ear and looked at his mom. "Can I keep him?" he asked.

Mrs. Hollinger hesitated.

"You've been promising for, like, a year," Courtney added.

"Yeah, Mom," Adam agreed.

"Courtney, you and Adam are actually agreeing on something?"

Courtney blushed. "He's still my dumb brother," she said. "But we've been talking about getting a dog for a while. You kept saying as soon as we were old enough to be responsible, we could get one. And no one's more responsible than my dorky brother."

Mrs. Hollinger couldn't help but smile. "I only worry about Dad. He's been hesitant about getting a dog — or any pet for that matter."

"I can text him," Courtney suggested.

"Courtney, you know he hates text messages."

Mrs. Hollinger closed her eyes and took a deep breath. She looked at Adam again and blinked at the tears in the corner of her son's eyes.

"Oh, all right," she said after a good long while. "I just hope Dad doesn't get too upset."

Adam smiled while Courtney's fingers flew a mile a minute. She took a picture of the puppy and texted the news to Aileen.

Corgi Capers: Deceit on Dorset Drive

While Three met his new Person, Four grew wilder and wilder. She ran back and forth in the pen barking, and she kept barreling into One.

"You know," Grandma Pickwick said. "These dogs sometimes like to live in pairs."

"What do you mean?" Mrs. Hollinger asked.

Grandma Pickwick pointed at Courtney, who was absorbed in her texting. "It's also sometimes beneficial for each child to have a pet of her own."

Mrs. Hollinger caught her meaning. "Courtney, why don't you look at the puppies and see if maybe another one might be right for us?"

Courtney rolled her eyes. "'Cuz my stupid brother already picked one."

Nonetheless, she walked to the puppies' pen. One was sitting in the middle of the pen, keeping a cautious eye on Four, who was still running wildly about.

"That puppy's been a challenge," Grandpa admitted. "She's got a lot of spunk."

As Courtney approached, Four's energy seemed to grow and grow. She kept charging at One. To avoid her, One scurried to the other end of the pen. His tail darted down; his ears flattened back. Even so, Four continued to charge. She built up so much speed that as she approached One, she couldn't stop. Instead, she leaped right on top of One, using him as a springboard to jump free of the pen.

"Stop!" Grandpa called, but Four didn't even slow down.

"Come back!" Grandma yelled, but Four ignored her pleas.

She made wide circles around the lawn. In Adam's arms, Three growled softly at his sister. Owl had gotten down off the porch to watch, and even Sparkles barked from the kitchen window.

For once, Courtney was not sending text messages. Instead, she seemed entranced watching the puppy run circles around the minivan, the puppy pen, and the group of people. Finally, Four let out a little squeak and jumped, full-speed, into Courtney's arms.

Courtney could do nothing but catch the squirming puppy. Everyone looked at her, startled that she had managed to catch the wildest of the corgis. They watched as the little puppy showered her with kisses. Then Courtney did something she rarely did when she wasn't surrounded by Aileen and her other friends: she smiled.

"When a puppy has chosen its master," Grandpa Pickwick said. "There's really no arguing about it. You'd better take the little one home with you, too. No charge."

"No charge?" Mrs. Hollinger asked.

"No," said Grandpa. "Knowing she has found the right person is payment enough."

Courtney approached her brother. They both held their new puppies, and they looked at each other with silent smiles.

Corgi Capers: Deceit on Dorset Drive

"Well." Mrs. Hollinger sighed. "I'm sure Dad will be waiting."

"That's the problem." Adam looked at his mother knowingly.

"He's gonna freak out," Courtney added, hiding a giggle.

Grandma and Grandpa pet the puppies once more. From the front porch, where he was lounging again, Owl gave two happy barks.

As Adam and Courtney carried Three and Four to the van, the puppies peeked over the shoulders of their new People. There, they saw One sitting lonely in his pen. One seemed smaller and smaller and smaller as they got further away.

"What do you think will happen to One?" Four asked quietly, but Three didn't want to answer when his People could hear. Owl and Sparkles had always been careful about that. Instead, he gave his sister a look that quieted her for now.

Inside the van, Adam checked that Patrick's comic book was tucked carefully in the magazine holder behind the front seat. He then sat down, buckled himself in, and held little Three on his lap. The dog sat quietly, sniffing the new smell of the van. Occasionally, for no reason at all, he would wag his tail, turn around, and lick Adam's face.

When Adam was situated, Courtney held out little Four. "Here, you think you can hold her for a minute?"

Corgi Capers: Deceit on Dorset Drive

Adam frowned. He had seen how rambunctious Four had been when she got loose
from her pen. He wasn't sure he could hold
both puppies at once.

"Here, Stupid," Courtney said.

Adam took the dog. She whined and
squirmed. She reminded Adam of a fish out of
water, flipping and flopping in all directions.
She squirmed so much that she knocked her
brother onto the floor. This seemed to delight
her, and she barked happily. Adam had to use
most of his energy to keep her from jumping
onto the floor and out the open minivan door.

In the meantime, Courtney was busy
moving her enormous shopping bags into the
front seat.

*"Probably doesn't want the dogs to pee
on her new clothes,"* Adam thought. *"Always
thinking about herself. She'll probably make
me hold both dogs while she texts on her cell
phone the whole ride back."*

But to Adam's surprise, when Courtney
was finished clearing her shopping bags, she
climbed into the back seat and sat down next
to Adam.

"I just figured," Courtney said to Adam's look of surprise, "that the puppies would
probably want to sit together."

Courtney didn't even have time to re-
trieve her puppy from Adam's lap before Four
jumped into her arms.

"She sure likes you," Adam said as
Three snuggled back into Adam's lap.

"Well, he likes you." Courtney nodded to Three.

"You think Mom will know how to get home?"

Both of them looked out the open door of the minivan.

"I think the Pickwicks gave her directions." At the farmhouse, Mrs. Hollinger was pointing to a piece of paper.

"She's probably correcting their grammar," Courtney joked.

Adam laughed and then returned his gaze to the puppies. "What are you going to name yours?"

"I hadn't thought about it. I was busy wondering how mad Dad's going to be. What are you naming your puppy?"

"I'm going to name him after Logan Zephyr."

"Logan *who*?"

"Logan Zephyr. The comic book hero."

Courtney returned his explanation with a blank stare.

"The space explorer. Remember? In the car ride just a few minutes ago I told you about him? There's a princess who reminds me of you. Princess Sapphire. The one who lives in the Sapphire Kingdom. She controls everything and always gets her way and..."

"I remember now," Courtney said. "Comic book nerd," she added.

"So anyway, I thought I'd name my dog after Logan Zephyr. I'm going to call him

Corgi Capers: Deceit on Dorset Drive

Zeph."

Three barked.

"You like that, boy?" Adam asked. "Your name is Zeph."

Again, the puppy barked and wagged his stubby tail.

"How about you?" Adam asked.

Courtney thought. "Hmmm. Maybe I should name her after that princess. The one from your story."

"Princess Sapphire?"

"Yes."

"I thought you hated comic books."

"Any character that annoys you is fine with me. Besides, I like the name — Princess Sapphire."

"It's a fancy name for a dog."

Courtney mused. "I could shorten it, like you did. Maybe I could call her Princess Sapphie. Or just Sapphie for short."

"Sapphie," Adam repeated. "I like it."

"Your name is Sapphie," Courtney told her puppy. "Princess Sapphie."

This sent Sapphie into another round of hysterical barking and fidgeting. She wagged her tail so hard her entire body wiggled from side to side. Hearing the word "princess," Zeph's ears perked up, and he joined his sister in her excitement, letting out a tiny howl. Adam and Courtney couldn't help but laugh.

A moment later, Mrs. Hollinger climbed into the driver's seat. "I have directions," she told her children. "And the Pickwicks even

Corgi Capers: Deceit on Dorset Drive

wrote down care instructions for the puppies and the location of a nearby pet shop. We can pick up food and water bowls, beds and toys..."

"Mom," Adam said, "We named our puppies."

"Did you? What are their names?"

"Zeph," Adam exclaimed.

"And Princess Sapphie."

Adam explained the origin of the names to his mother. "I can show you the comic book, but later. It's Patrick's copy, and I can't get it wrinkled. Or chewed up. It's a limited edition." He patted the comic book, which was nestled safely in the magazine holder. Sapphie watched his hand, sniffing at the comic book and licking her lips.

"No," Adam told her. Sapphie responded with another round of wild barking.

"Shhhh." Courtney patted Sapphie and the puppy immediately quieted, snuggling into her Person's lap.

"I think those are great names." Mrs. Hollinger smiled. "Oh, I almost forgot. Courtney, Missus Pickwick found this on the ground near the puppy pen. Looks like you dropped it when you caught Sapphie."

Mrs. Hollinger held up a pink phone decorated in purple rhinestones.

"My cell phone," Courtney cried.

"Wow!" Adam teased. "That's probably the longest you've been without it since — ever."

Corgi Capers: Deceit on Dorset Drive

Courtney took the phone from her mother without so much as a *thank you* and immediately started texting Aileen. But every time she tried to type something, Sapphie would jump up and distract her.

"Adam, can you hold her for a min — ?" Courtney asked.

But she saw that Adam had his hands full with Zeph. So with a sigh, she slipped her cell phone into her pocket and focused her energies on petting Sapphie — and keeping her as still as possible.

"Well," Mrs. Hollinger said from the front seat. "We've got directions, we've got puppies... there's just one problem."

She made eye contact with Adam in the rear view mirror, and the three of them answered in unison: "Dad."

As Mrs. Hollinger pulled down the bumpy driveway, they passed another car. In the back seat was a young girl, her face pressed hopefully against the window, eagerly looking towards the puppy pen.

Mrs. Hollinger tried the GPS one last time. "That's odd," she said. "It's working now — good as new."

The GPS turned on, and its computerized voice led the way to the pet store. As she drove, Mrs. Hollinger repeated Farmer Pickwick's words of wisdom.

"Maybe there's no such thing as a coincidence after all," she whispered and drove into the summer afternoon.

~ ELEVEN ~
Trouble Ahead

Adam and Courtney stood inside the pet shop staring at an entire wall of pet beds. Their shopping cart nearly overflowed with supplies: crates, food, bowls, collars, leashes, toys...

Sapphie squirmed and cried in Courtney's arms, struggling to break free. Her nose twitched in frustration. She wanted to investigate the display of very smelly ferrets in the middle of the pet shop.

"Sapphie, stop!" Courtney turned to Adam. "Let's hurry up. I'm not sure how much longer I can hold her."

"All we need now are beds," Adam said. Zeph squirmed in his arms, eager to reach a squirrel toy he saw in the shopping cart.

Mrs. Hollinger held her forehead. "If these puppies don't settle down by the time we get home, Dad's going to be really mad." Just then, her cell phone rang. She looked at the screen. "Speaking of Dad, he's calling now."

A knot tightened in Adams' stomach. Courtney frowned. What would Dad say when he found out they were in the pet shop? Even Zeph froze as if he, too, sensed something ominous.

Corgi Capers: Deceit on Dorset Drive

"I'd better take this call outside. Here's some money to pay for the supplies." She started to give Courtney a handful of bills but changed her mind and gave them to Adam instead.

"Stupid." Courtney stuck her tongue out at Adam after their mother left. "Give me the money. I'm older."

Sapphie squealed as Courtney grabbed the money out of her brother's hand.

Adam was too nervous to argue. The more time he spent with Zeph, the more he wanted to keep him. But Adam had a horrible feeling his dad wouldn't feel the same way.

He forced himself to focus on picking out a dog bed. He chose a yellow and red cushion shaped like a rocket ship. "It's perfect for a puppy that's named after a space explorer," he explained, trying to sound cheerful to hide his nerves.

"I prefer the kind of bed with sides," Courtney said, eyeing a fluffy pink one.

"What about this one?" Adam pointed to a powder blue bed with the word "princess" written in dark blue on the cushion.

"I like how it says *princess*," Courtney said thoughtfully. "After all, she *is* named Princess Sapphire, but I wish it were pink."

"Why? Blue is perfect for Sapphie."

"Blue?"

"A sapphire is a type of blue gem."

Courtney shot him a mean look. "Yeah, right. Sapphire is a type of pinkish-red."

Corgi Capers: Deceit on Dorset Drive

"Is not. It's blue. Princess Sapphire rules over the Sapphire Kingdom. It's paved in blue jewels," Adam insisted.

"I don't believe you. I'm going to text Aileen and ask her."

Adam shook his head. "You can't text while you're holding Sapphie. Ask Mom instead."

"Mom's on the phone."

"Well, it's right there on the front of Patrick's comic book. Go to the car and check."

Courtney glared at her brother. "It's pink," she insisted, but she took Sapphie outside to check.

"Be careful with the comic book," Adam called after her. "It's a limited edition!"

While she was gone, Adam turned to Zeph. It was nice to spend time with him alone without the distractions of Mom, Courtney, or Sapphie. Zeph's deep brown eyes stared up at him.

"I want to keep you so badly," Adam told the puppy. "You and Sapphie *have* to behave when we get home. Otherwise, Dad might not let us keep you."

Zeph cocked his head as if trying to understand what Adam was saying.

"Will you be good?"

Zeph howled gently and kissed Adam's hand.

Corgi Capers: Deceit on Dorset Drive

"Here." Adam pointed to a display of dog training books. "Maybe I can read up on training and teach you two how to be good."

Zeph snuggled into Adam's arm as Adam browsed through a book. He was just getting into the chapter on housebreaking when Courtney interrupted him.

"Fine, Nerd. *Sapphire* is blue."
Adam looked up and smiled. Was Courtney actually admitting he'd been right? But what he saw made his smile fade.

"You can't hold it like that!"

Courtney had Sapphie in her right hand and was dangling Patrick's comic book by the cover from her left.

"It's just a stupid comic book," she said.

On the other side of the pet shop, a parrot squawked, and Sapphie struggled to get free.

"Sapphie, no," Courtney shouted.

She needed both hands to control the rambunctious puppy, and Adam cringed as he heard the comic book cover tear. Courtney dropped it, and it fell to the floor in a crunch of paper.

Adam placed Zeph in the shopping cart and carefully picked up the comic book. Zeph, sitting on top of a bag of dog food, wagged his tail and finally bit into the squirrel toy. Adam smoothed out the pages.

"Patrick will never forgive me," he told Courtney, pushing the torn edges together.

Corgi Capers: Deceit on Dorset Drive

She shrugged, took the blue princess bed from the shelf, and threw it into the cart, nearly knocking Zeph over.

"This is Patrick's limited edition comic book," Adam repeated, steadying Zeph. "He'll be mad it's ruined."

"Not my problem." Courtney shrugged again.

Adam gave the comic book another look. He hoped Patrick wouldn't mind that the cover was torn. His sister was so careless. It was hard to believe he was actually related to her.

Adam placed the comic book on top of the dog bed and pushed the cart, keeping a careful eye on both Zeph and the comic book. Zeph seemed content with the squirrel toy, but Sapphie squirmed each time he squeaked it.

"Stop, Sapphie," Courtney scolded. Sapphie quieted, but her eyes remained locked on the squirrel.

Courtney turned to Adam. "We might as well pay for all this. Mom's still outside on the phone. I don't know what she's talking about, but it sounds serious."

"What kind of serious?" Adam asked.

Courtney shrugged.

"Okay. Let me hold Sapphie, and you can pay."

"Can you handle two puppies at once? After all, you're only a fourth grader."

Corgi Capers: Deceit on Dorset Drive

"I'm starting *fifth grade*," Adam reminded her. "And of course I can handle two
puppies."

Courtney laughed. She loved torment-
ing her brother.

"Give me Sapphie."

Courtney handed the puppy to her
brother. With a yelp, she jumped into Adam's
arms, bounced off of him, and landed in the
shopping cart. She lunged at Zeph, grabbing
his squirrel toy. The two puppies growled.
Customers stared. Sapphie fought so hard for
the squirrel that both puppies nearly fell out
of the cart.

A silver-haired woman passed down the
aisle. "Oh, that'll be a stubborn one." She
stopped a moment and leaned down over Sapphie.

Sapphie dropped the squirrel, looked
right at the woman, and gave a shrill, ear-
piercing bark.

"How do you know she'll be stubborn?"
Adam asked the woman.

He handed Sapphie back over to Courtney before the puppies started fighting again.

"You can tell by her markings."

"Her markings?" Courtney asked.

"Yes. See how this puppy's white markings are symmetrical?" The old woman pointed to Zeph's face. The white, triangular patch
on Zeph's forehead ran evenly down his nose
and covered both jowls.

"Yes."

Corgi Capers: Deceit on Dorset Drive

"Well," she told Courtney, "your dog's white markings are only on one side of her face."

Courtney and Adam compared the puppies: indeed, Sapphie's triangular marking only covered the left side of her face, covering her jaw, muzzle, and left eye. The other side of her face was brown.

"I never really noticed that before," Adam said.

"It's a sign there's something off-balance about her personality. Just like Jennie, the beagle I had growing up. You're going to have your hands full with that one."

"Uh, thanks... I think," Courtney said.

She struggled to control Sapphie and sheepishly handed her brother the money so he could pay for the overflowing cart of puppy supplies.

Corgi Capers: Deceit on Dorset Drive

~ TWELVE ~
The Burglar Strikes Again

Outside, Mrs. Hollinger was still on the phone. She paced back and forth in front of the store, and her brow was drawn up with lines of worry.

"Hold on, here are the kids." She lowered her cell phone. "It's Dad. He has some bad news."

Courtney and Adam braced themselves. Mrs. Hollinger looked upset.

"Mom must have told Dad about the puppies," Courtney whispered.

"Maybe he won't let us keep them," Adam whispered back.

He looked down at Zeph, who wagged his little tail and kissed Adam's hand. Adam thought of all the ideas he had for training the puppies. He thought of how fun it would be for Zeph to watch him at baseball games. He thought of the cartful of supplies he couldn't wait to use. How disappointed he'd be if he had to give it all back!

"Dad is very upset right now," Mrs. Hollinger explained.

Adam and Courtney exchanged nervous glances. Since he ran his own business, Mr. Hollinger was always worried about conserving money. Maybe he thought having two puppies would be too expensive. Adam fought a pit in his stomach.

"I'll use my savings to pay for these supplies," Adam blurted. "Even Courtney's!"

"Me too!" Courtney said, forgetting that she'd just spent all her money at the mall.

Their mother frowned.

"I promise I'll clean up after them," Adam pleaded.

"And I promise I'll be responsible," Courtney added.

Mrs. Hollinger shook her head. "It's not the puppies."

Adam breathed a sigh of relief.

"I haven't even told him about Sapphie or Zeph."

"What's he upset about, then?" Courtney asked.

Mrs. Hollinger sighed. "Dad came back from his meeting and found our house was broken into." A tear streamed down her cheek.

Adam gasped, forgetting all about the puppies for a moment.

"The worst part is that Dad's office was trashed. His work computer was stolen. That computer had all his blueprints on it. Worse, it had clients' personal information. The police are worried that the burglar might be an identity thief. Now all Dad's clients are at risk. This is really bad for his business."

Mrs. Hollinger covered up the mouthpiece of her cell phone. "I didn't think it was

Corgi Capers: Deceit on Dorset Drive

the right time to tell him about the puppies," she added.

"You have to tell him, Mom," Adam pleaded.

"I'm not going to tell him now. He'll find out when we get home."

But Adam insisted. "If you tell him now, he'll have time to get used to the idea."

For once, Courtney agreed with her brother. "Please! I really want to keep Sapphie."

Sapphie barked at Mrs. Hollinger. Zeph howled.

"I don't know," Mrs. Hollinger said, offering her son the phone. "Maybe *you* should tell him."

Adam put the phone to his ear and started speaking without knowing quite what to say.

"Dad," he mumbled in a shaky voice. "I'm sorry about your computer... but I have to tell you something." He wasn't sure he could continue, but Zeph nuzzled his hand. "The reason we're so late coming home is that we're at the pet store buying dog supplies."

Adam swallowed hard and continued. "On the way home we got lost and ran into a family selling dogs. Corgis."

"So you got a dog?" Mr. Hollinger's tired voice asked.

"No," Adam explained.

Mr. Hollinger breathed a sigh of relief.

Corgi Capers: Deceit on Dorset Drive

"That is," Adam corrected, "we got two dogs."

Mr. Hollinger groaned. In the background, Adam heard the doorbell ring.

"That's the police," Mr. Hollinger said. "I've got to go. We'll talk about this later."

"Are you mad, Dad?"

"Yes," Mr. Hollinger said, "and no."

The phone went silent.

"How did he take it?" Mrs. Hollinger asked.

"I don't know."

Adam patted Zeph on the head, hoping he wouldn't have to give up his puppy. Deep down, a part of him felt like crying.

"Well," Courtney said. "At least Dad has time to think about it before we get home."

In the minivan, the dogs fidgeted on Courtney's and Adam's laps.

"Maybe they want to sleep in their beds," Courtney suggested.

Adam reached back to the second row of seats and placed Zeph on the rocket ship bed. Courtney placed Sapphie in the blue princess bed. The dogs quieted immediately and curled up into little fur balls.

"Guess they're tired," Adam said.

For a few minutes, everyone sat quietly. Even Mrs. Hollinger drove in silence. The puppies had distracted them from the news of the burglary, but now that they were sleeping, Adam and Courtney would have to face

Corgi Capers: Deceit on Dorset Drive

the sad reality that their house had been burglarized.

It was Courtney who finally broke the
silence. "So Mom, what was...stolen?"

Mrs. Hollinger pulled up to a red light
and turned to look her daughter in the eye.
The late afternoon sun shone in, accenting
her sad face and watery eyes.

"They took your jewelry, Courtney. Adam, they took some of your video games.
They took my jewelry as well, and a stack of
money I had in my sock drawer. They threw a
bunch of books and clothes on the floor looking for hidden valuables. And they ransacked
your father's office."

Adam frowned. Mr. Hollinger worked
out of a home office, a detached garage that
had been converted into a suite for his archi-
tectural business. Even though he tended to
be messy, he made a special effort to keep his
workplace absolutely spotless. Everything was
organized in file cabinets. Blueprints were
rolled and stored. Adam tried to imagine what
the office must look like now.

"Dad must be devastated."

"He is," Mrs. Hollinger explained. "Especially about his computer. It isn't even
worth all that much."

"Except to an identity thief," Adam
muttered. "Weren't the police just next door
at the Pinkneys' house? Why would the burglar
strike twice in one day?"

"Maybe he thought no one would expect it," Mrs. Hollinger mused.

"That's true," Adam agreed. "Very sneaky."

In the meantime, Courtney fell back into her routine of sending dozens of text messages to her friends. Only this time as her fingers flew across the keyboard, she wasn't smiling.

In the back seat, Zeph climbed into Sapphie's bed and curled up right next to her. Softly, the two puppies whispered to each other.

"A store," Zeph said. "What a strange place. Very different from Pickwick Farm."

Sapphie didn't seem to hear. "Did you hear what that old woman said about me? The nerve! Saying that I'm unbalanced! What do you think, Three?"

"Sapphie, my name is Zeph. Remem - ber?"

"Fine. What do you think about what that old woman said, Three? I mean, Zeph?"

Zeph sighed. "Just ignore her. We've got more important things to worry about."

"What could be more important that that woman's insult? There's nothing unbalanced about me!"

Zeph tried to ignore his sister. "Didn't you hear what our People said?"

"I'll tell you what I *did* hear! That strange blue bird in the corner of the store. It

Corgi Capers: Deceit on Dorset Drive

sounded like this: *Squawk! Squawk! Squawk!* Boy I'd like to smell *that* bird up close. *Squawk! Squawk! Squawk!*" Sapphie squealed again, imitating the bird.

Zeph rolled his eyes.

Courtney turned around. "Sapphie, shhhh!"

Sapphie stood up, wagged her tail, and barked at Courtney before settling back down into her bed.

After a moment, Zeph spoke to her.

"Focus, Sapphie. I'm really worried."

"Why?"

"Something bad has happened at our new home, and we're going to make it worse."

"How?"

"I don't know. Someone named 'Dad' had something very important taken from him today. And my Person thinks he's upset that we're moving into his house. Maybe the whole thing is our fault."

"What can we do?" Sapphie asked.

"I don't know. I don't understand exactly what's happening. But I do know that our People are upset. We have to find a way to help."

"Nonsense," Sapphie said. "Everyone thinks I'm so cute. I'll cheer them up. Just watch and see. Let me meet this 'Dad' person and see how he melts in my paw. He'll think I'm the cutest dog he's ever seen!"

Zeph shook his head at his sister's confidence, hoping there was some truth to it.

~ * ~

As the minivan pulled into the family's driveway, Adam and Courtney put aside their disagreements from earlier that day and shared a nervous glance.

Mr. Hollinger sat on the front porch with Mr. and Mrs. Pinkney. When the minivan came to a stop, Mr. Hollinger got up and shuffled toward the van. His shoulders were hunched over, his eyes cast downwards.

Adam held his breath. Courtney silenced her cell phone. In the back seat of the minivan, the two puppies whimpered.

"You think we'll be allowed to keep the dogs?" Adam asked.

Courtney frowned and whispered sadly to her brother. "I wouldn't count on it."

Corgi Capers: Deceit on Dorset Drive

~ THIRTEEN ~
Four-legged Levity

From Adam and Courtney's perspec-
tive, Mr. Hollinger seemed to move in slow
motion.

"What if he's mad?" Courtney asked.
"What if he tells us we have to send the puppies back?"

*"Mom would never be able to find her
way back to Pickwick Farm,"* Adam wanted to
say, but he knew it was no time for jokes.

Adam and Courtney sat as still as possible. They watched Mr. Hollinger grow closer-
closer-closer. Adam swallowed hard, closed
his eyes, and took a deep breath. When he
opened his eyes, Mr. Hollinger was opening
the side door of the minivan.

At first he said nothing. He just stared
at Adam, Courtney, and the puppies. Zeph
cried and dashed under the seat. Sapphie
leapt off of Courtney's lap and jumped onto
Adam, who sat furthest from the door — and
furthest from Mr. Hollinger.

Adam tried to read the stern look on his
father's face without quite making eye contact. Mr. Hollinger's brow wrinkled with worry.

Adam glanced at Courtney. Her cell
phone vibrated, but she didn't dare move to
answer it.

"Hi Dad," she said so quietly it was almost a whisper.

Mr. Hollinger nodded and looked at Adam.

"Hi Dad," Adam whispered a little too quickly.

Mr. Hollinger nodded and turned to Sapphie. She squirmed on Adam's lap and trembled.

"Hmmm," Mr. Hollinger groaned.

At that, Sapphie let out the tiniest squeak, and Adam tried very hard to stay still as he felt a stream of warm liquid trickle onto his lap. He dared not complain in front of his father and was relieved when Mr. Hollinger redirected his gaze to Zeph, whose tiny head poked out from underneath the seat.

Finally, Mr. Hollinger closed his eyes and took a deep breath. When he opened them again, he was smiling.

"Hi kids," he said finally. His voice sounded more tired than mad. "Hi puppies," he added. "I'm glad the three of you stopped at the farm. I'd hate to think of what could have happened if you'd been home when the burglar struck."

Zeph emerged from under the seat, and both puppies wagged their tails.

Adam looked at his sister in shock.

"Come on!" said Mr. Hollinger, clapping his hands.

Zeph jumped out of the minivan and followed Mr. Hollinger. Sapphie followed her

Corgi Capers: Deceit on Dorset Drive

brother, jumping off of Adam's lap to reveal the tiny wet spot.

"That was close," Adam whispered.

But now that Mr. Hollinger was out of hearing range, Courtney was focused on just one thing. Her lips curled in a smile, and she pulled out her cell phone and took a picture of the wet spot on Adam's lap.

"Ha ha!" she laughed. "It looks like you wet yourself! Aileen and Marnie will love this picture."

Adam scowled. "That's not fair. It was *your* dog that peed on my lap."

But Courtney just laughed as she sent the picture.

"Come on, kids!" Mr. Hollinger said from the driveway. "Mister and Missus Pinkney would like to meet your puppies. We've had a rough day and could use some cheering up."

"Courtney, don't send that picture," Adam pleaded. But it was too late. The message had been sent.

Now Aileen and Marnie Ellison would send the picture to half of the kids at school, and Adam would be the laughing-stock once again. As he followed his sister to the front porch, at least he could be happy about one thing: when it came to the puppies, Dad didn't seem to be mad at all.

On the porch, Mr. and Mrs. Pinkney sat on the wrought-iron bench. Mrs. Pinkney smiled and called to the dogs. Sapphie jumped wildly, her tongue licking at the air. She tried to jump on Mrs. Pinkney's lap, but her legs were too short so she paced back and forth, whining in frustration.

Zeph greeted the Pinkneys hesitantly, being sure to stay close to Adam the whole time. Finally, he sat at Mrs. Pinkney's feet, tail wagging as she rubbed his head. Seeing her opportunity, Sapphie backed up, yelped, and sprinted down the porch headed straight for Zeph. She used him as a ramp, springing up his back and leaping directly onto Mr. Pinkney's lap.

Adam swallowed hard, wondering how the stern Mr. Pinkney would react to the wild and wiggling puppy.

But even Mr. Pinkney smiled. "They're very cute," he admitted.

Before long, everyone had forgotten — at least for the time being — about the burglaries. The puppies stumbled happily from one person to the next. Each time he met someone new, Zeph gave a little high-pitched howl that reminded Adam of Owl. Even Mr. Hollinger was petting them.

Finally, they settled down. Zeph lay at Adam's feet and Sapphie jumped into Courtney's cross-legged lap.

"So Dad, you're not mad?" Adam asked. "On the phone you said you were."

"I'm not mad about the puppies," Mr. Hollinger said. "I was upset about our house... and my computer. I'm not looking forward to

Corgi Capers: Deceit on Dorset Drive

calling my clients and letting them know their personal information was stolen."

"We were worried," Courtney said after sending a text message. "We thought you'd make us take them back."

"I'm glad you two got puppies." Mr. Hollinger smiled tiredly. "You've wanted a dog for a long time now. But they're *your* dogs. It's your job to feed them, walk them, brush them...I don't mind if *you* have puppies. But I won't have a thing to do with them." He looked down at the corgis and tried to hide a smile.

Adam eyed the drying spot on his pants. "I was reading up on housebreaking," he said.

Mrs. Hollinger smiled. "Let's hope you're successful."

For a moment everyone went quiet. Nothing could be heard but the lonely sound of crickets and the eerie whisper of the wind through the summer leaves.

Adam turned to the Pinkneys. "I'm sorry about your house."

"And I'm sorry about yours," Mrs. Pinkney replied.

"Eden," Mr. Hollinger said. "Tell them about the ring the thief took."

Mrs. Pinkney nodded. "The worst thing the burglar took was my grandmother's ring." She spoke as if in a trance as she recited the description of the ring. "It was white gold, hand crafted with embellishments that looked

like swirling waves of the ocean, and six amethysts set in the waves. Inside the ring, my
grandfather engraved something: *the ocean
eternal, like our love.* He gave it to my
grandmother a long time ago. I hope I can get
it back."

"That's so sad," Courtney said.

Staring into the distance, each person
seemed lost in their own thoughts. Out of nowhere, both corgis let out a single, shrill bark.

"What's wrong?" Adam asked.

Everyone looked around to find the
cause of the puppies' alarm.

"Oh," Mr. Hollinger said after a moment. "That's just old Mr. Frostburg."

He pointed at a man hobbling down the
street with a cane.

"Good evening, neighbors," Mr. Frostburg shouted from the street. "How're you?"

"We've been better, Jim," Mr. Hollinger shouted back.

"I'm sorry." Mr. Frostburg pulled his
baseball cap down over his eyes. "Anything I
can do to help?"

"Not unless you know how to catch a
burglar," Mr. Hollinger answered.

"What?" Mr. Frostburg limped toward
the porch, leaning on his cane for support.

Zeph cried and hid behind Adam.

"It's okay." Adam stroked his puppy's
back. "It's just old Mister Frostburg."

"What's this about a burglary?" asked
Mr. Frostburg once he reached the porch.

Corgi Capers: Deceit on Dorset Drive

Before anyone could stop her, Sapphie dashed out from behind Courtney and grabbed a hold of Mr. Frostburg's cane. Zeph barked.

"Zeph!" Adam shouted.

"Sapphie!" Courtney shouted.

Sapphie wouldn't release her grip on the cane.

"That's the trouble with puppies." Mr. Hollinger grabbed both dogs by the scruff of their necks. "Where are their collars, any-way?"

"Too bad you didn't have the dogs *yes-terday*," Mr. Frostburg said. "They might have scared away your burglar."

But only Adam heard him over the pup-pies' barking.

"I don't think they've ever seen a man with a cane before," Adam tried to explain.

Mr. Hollinger frowned. "Kids, bring the puppies into the back yard. We're trying to have an adult conversation here, and they're being rude."

Adam nodded, scooping up both pup-pies. Courtney finished sending a text before following her brother and the puppies into the fenced-in back yard.

"Sorry, Jim. We've had a rough day. Two burglaries and two puppies all at once." Mr. Hollinger held his forehead.

"I'm sorry to hear it," Mr. Frostburg said. "Were many things stolen?"

Corgi Capers: Deceit on Dorset Drive

Mrs. Pinkney sighed. "Our house was ransacked."

"I'm sorry, Eden. But you did have homeowner's insurance, right? Won't your insurance replace the things that were stolen?"

"Yes. But they can't replace my grandmother's ring." Once again, Mrs. Pinkney recited the description of the ring.

"Hmmm. It sounds like it was a lovely ring. My condolences. And you?" he asked, looking at Mr. and Mrs. Hollinger.

Mr. Hollinger sighed. "They got some jewelry and video games. But most important is my office computer with all my important files."

Mr. Frostburg nodded. "It must be that serial burglar. He's been hitting all the houses in the neighborhood, hasn't he? I'd better use extra lights from now on. Wouldn't want *my* house to be burglarized, too."

"Good idea," Mrs. Hollinger agreed.

"You know," Mr. Pinkney said. "Someone ought to warn the Stoys."

Mrs. Hollinger looked at Mr. Hollinger. Mr. Hollinger looked at Mrs. Pinkney. Mrs. Pinkney looked at her husband.

"Just a thought." Mr. Pinkney shrugged. "I mean, *somebody* ought to warn them."

"You can warn them if you like," Mrs. Pinkney said. "But those two are so grumpy, I'd hate for them to start screaming at us just for ringing their doorbell."

"The last time I went over there, I was bringing over a piece of mail that had been accidentally delivered to our house," Mr. Hollinger explained. "It was only around four, but Missus Stoy yelled at me for interrupting during dinnertime. I felt like a helpless child."

Mr. Frostburg smiled. "I don't mind talking to them. I'll go warn them. I'll even offer to check their windows and doors to make sure their house is burglar-proof."

"That's nice of you," Mrs. Hollinger said.

"Better you than us," Mr. Pinkney added.

"It's nothing. I'm sure you all have more important things to do anyway. And I'm sorry for your loss."

Mr. Frostburg waved and turned slowly toward the Stoys' house.

From the back yard, Zeph and Adam watched Mr. Frostburg limp up the hill to the Stoys' driveway. A moment later, an elderly figure opened the door, and Mr. Frostburg disappeared inside.

Adam shuddered. "Poor Mr. Frostburg. I hope the Stoys go easy on him!"

Adam had had more than one run-in with the Stoys. Just the other day, they had yelled at him for playing catch too close to their front lawn. He and Patrick had been playing in the street, and the Stoys sat out on their front porch as if they were scrutinizing the game. Each time the ball landed on their lawn, Mr. Stoy gave them a dirty look and said they were ruining his grass.

Courtney was too busy texting to notice Mr. Frostburg, or Adam for that matter. She was also too busy to notice that Sapphie had bitten off a small piece of the rubber stopper on Mr. Frostburg's cane. Courtney didn't even notice when Sapphie dug a small hole and buried the piece of rubber in the backyard and was so pleased with herself she looked like she was smiling.

~ FOURTEEN ~
The Messiest Room in the House

That evening, everyone — even Mr. and Mrs. Pinkney — helped carry the puppy supplies into the Hollingers' house. They were happy to have something to do besides sit and worry about their burglarized homes.

Mrs. Pinkney helped Courtney set up the puppies' crates in the kitchen while Mrs. Hollinger brought their dog beds into the family room. Mr. Hollinger and Mr. Pinkney helped Adam check the backyard for any weak spots in the fence that might allow the puppies to run away.

Before long, everything was set up, the puppies had been fed, and everyone was left with nothing to do.

"We should put the puppies in their crates," Mr. Hollinger suggested. "We've got to take a good look at what's been stolen."

Adam gently picked up Zeph. "Time to go in your crate."

He placed the puppy on the cushion inside his crate, handed Zeph a biscuit, and gently closed and latched the door. Zeph looked up at him, confused.

Courtney did the same for Sapphie. Sapphie looked at Courtney, then at her brother. No one seemed upset, which put Sapphie at ease. She gobbled up her biscuit, turned around three times, and plopped down into the plush cushion. Almost immediately, her eyes closed.

"We should leave you all alone now," Mrs. Pinkney said.

"No," Adam insisted.

He tried to remember how his favorite detectives spoke in comic books.

"We need you to see if there's anything familiar. Maybe the burglar has a specific pattern or left a clue. In my comic books, the detectives say things like that may help catch the criminal."

"All right." Mrs. Pinkney smiled at Adam's initiative.

The six of them walked slowly through the house. In the living room, the drawers from the coffee table had been yanked out and emptied. A deck of playing cards was scattered along the rug, and some pewter coasters lay on the hardwood floor. One of the drawers had been tossed at the fireplace, and the brick hearth left a huge gash in the wood.

"What a shame." Mrs. Hollinger rubbed the drawer.

"The burglar was just as careless with our things, too," Mrs. Pinkney said. "He must be strong, tossing drawers like feathers."

"Strong," Adam noted.

Next, they walked through the dining room. The cabinet had been opened, and a few pieces of fallen china lay broken on the shelves and the floor below. The empty

Corgi Capers: Deceit on Dorset Drive

shelves indicated that some silverware — the fancy kind Mrs. Hollinger only used on holidays — had been stolen.

In the family room, Adam's collection of video games had been rummaged through. Most of them were gone, but a few were scattered on the rug. The family's DVD collection was missing.

"It's not so bad," Adam said, trying to sound brave.

"Let's go upstairs." Mrs. Hollinger put one hand on Courtney's shoulder and the other hand on Adam's.

At the door to her room, Courtney shrieked. Her dresser had been ransacked. All her clothes were on the floor. Her jewelry box had been turned upside-down, and her nicest pieces of jewelry were gone. Her eyes filled with tears, and she plopped down on her bed, her fingers flying across the keys of her cell phone.

"You okay, Court?" Mr. Hollinger asked. Courtney nodded, but she asked them to close the door on their way out.

"I need some time alone," she said.

Adam's room, mostly full of toys and books, was untouched. Luckily, the burglar hadn't checked his dresser: in his sock drawer he kept fifty dollars his grandmother had given him for his birthday last year.

Adam grabbed his old grey hat from his closet. It was a fedora, a dress hat that had belonged to his father, who used to wear it

Corgi Capers: Deceit on Dorset Drive

when he commuted into the city for work. Ever since he started working from home, Mr. Hollinger hadn't needed it. Adam liked to wear the hat while he read detective comic books. It made him feel like his favorite detective, Riley Couth the Super Sleuth.

Now, Adam donned the hat in hopes it would inspire him to solve the mystery of the serial burglar. He tilted it over his brow — the way Riley Couth wore it — and peeked into his parents' bedroom.

Mr. and Mrs. Hollinger's room looked a lot like Courtney's with the dressers ransacked and the jewelry taken.

Mrs. Hollinger took one look but sobbed and continued down the hall.

"I can't look at it just now," she muttered to Adam.

The Pinkneys lowered their eyes and followed. "It's the same mess the burglar left in our house," Mrs. Pinkney sighed.

Everyone followed Mrs. Hollinger to the only other room upstairs: Mr. Hollinger's junk room. It was the messiest room in the Hollinger household.

Mr. Hollinger loved to keep things. He hated getting rid of anything. Fortunately, he was the only one who used the room, for it contained so much junk only one person could fit inside.

Adam and Courtney weren't supposed to go in, and Mrs. Hollinger avoided it. Mr. Hollinger liked the fact that it belonged only

Corgi Capers: Deceit on Dorset Drive

to him, and he could keep it as messy as he liked.

The junk room wasn't that big to begin with, and every surface — the file cabinet, the loveseat, and the desk (not to mention the floor) — was covered in junk. Even the built-in bookshelves were full from end to end with college textbooks.

Next to the bookshelf was a large stack of newspapers. Mr. Hollinger read *The Wall Street Journal* every day, and he got the *Sunday Times* delivered on the weekend. He refused to recycle the newspapers until he had read them all, from the first page to the last. He sometimes ran out of time for this, and the unread newspapers ended up stacked in a tall pile. By now the stack was four or five feet high.

In addition to all this mess, there were cardboard boxes loaded with anything from old baseball helmets to papers he'd written back in high school. Some of the boxes were neatly stacked and sealed, but others were opened and overflowing.

On top of the file cabinet was a very old printer hooked up to an even older computer that sat on the desk. The computer's screen was tiny — all black with green font. The first time he showed it to the kids, they laughed at how old the technology was. It was nothing like their new computer in the family room.

When the Pinkneys peeked inside, they couldn't believe the clutter.

"Oh dear!" Mrs. Pinkney shrieked. "The burglar completely destroyed this room."

Mrs. Hollinger and Adam looked at each other. Sure, there were stacks of newspapers everywhere, and overflowing cardboard boxes. But they knew the truth: the room *always* looked like this. In fact, it was such a mess, even the burglar hadn't bothered to enter.

Mr. Hollinger laughed awkwardly in the hallway. Mrs. Hollinger laughed too, releasing the stress of the day. Before long, Adam joined in. They laughed so loudly, Courtney emerged from her room.

"What's so funny?"

Mrs. Hollinger managed to provide a brief explanation. "Missus Pinkney thinks the junk room was the hardest hit by the burglar."

"Because of the mess," Adam added.

Mrs. Hollinger exploded in another round of laughter.

Courtney stepped up to the door and looked around. "I don't know what you're talking about. It looks like always to me."

Mr. Hollinger looked sheepish for a moment. "I like to collect things," he admitted. "And this is the only place in the house Susan allows me to do that."

Mrs. Pinkney tried to remain composed, but after a while the tension of the day got to her as well, and before long she had joined

Corgi Capers: Deceit on Dorset Drive

Mrs. Hollinger, Adam, and Courtney in an un-
controllable fit of the giggles. After a minute,
even Mr. Hollinger and Mr. Pinkney found
themselves drawn in, relieving their stress
through a good laugh.

~ FIFTEEN ~
Escape Artists

Down in the kitchen, Zeph and Sapphie sat in their crates. Sapphie had curled up already, enjoying a little nap, but Zeph was wide-awake. His nose twitched as he sniffed all the kitchen smells, and his huge ears struggled to make sense of what he heard coming from upstairs.

"Does that sound like laughing to you?" he asked Sapphie.

She sat up sleepily. "I was just having the best nap. You shouldn't have woken me." She stretched slowly, then shook herself off. Finally, when she was seated again, she asked, "What were you saying?"

"I thought all of our People were upset. But it sounds like they're all laughing. Does that make any sense to you?"

"People *never* make sense to me. Like, why are we in these cages?"

"They're not cages. They're crates."

"Well why do we have to stay in them? I really liked that soft thing they let us sleep on in the car."

"Weren't you listening two nights ago?"

"No," Sapphie admitted. "What happened two nights ago?"

"You need to do a better job of listening. Remember when Ma and Pa were in the

Corgi Capers: Deceit on Dorset Drive

kitchen back at Pickwick Farm and told us to stay awake and listen to their advice?"

"They did? I don't remember that. I must have been sleeping."

"Well anyway, they told us about crates. They're like little caves we get to live in. People put us in here when they're away from home so we can't get into trouble."

"What kind of trouble could we possibly get into?" Sapphie asked innocently.

Zeph laughed. "I can think of one or two things. But don't you remember? They also taught us the secret way of getting out if we had to."

"Escaping?"

"Sort of, yes. They told us not to use it unless we really have to. If our People ever found out we knew how to escape, they'd make it much more difficult."

"Can you show me?" Sapphie asked, now fully alert.

Zeph raised his paw, reaching for the latch to the crate door. But his paw wouldn't reach. His stubby little legs were too short. "It's harder than when Pa explained it."

"Your paw's not high enough. You're too short." Sapphie tried her own paw, but she was even shorter.

"Try sitting up some," Zeph suggested.

Sapphie balanced carefully so she was seated on just her two hind legs. She raised her long body up so that her front paw was perfectly level with the latch to the crate.

Corgi Capers: Deceit on Dorset Drive

"You've almost got it," Zeph encouraged.

"Now what?"

"Push the latch up with your paw."

Sapphie did. "Now what?"

Zeph cocked his head, trying to remember what Pa Corgi told him. "Jiggle the latch with your teeth until it comes loose," he said finally.

Sapphie stuck her muzzle through the wire bars of the door and grasped the latch in her sharp puppy teeth.

Just then, the puppies heard six pair of feet coming down the stairs.

"Get down, Sapphie. Curl up and pretend to be sleeping!"

Sapphie did as her brother instructed.

"Well, goodnight," Mr. Pinkney said to the Hollingers as they walked past the kitchen and down the steps to the front door. "Let us know if you need anything. And good luck with those puppies."

Mrs. Pinkney stopped at the kitchen door. "They're so cute, all curled up and sleeping."

"They *are* cute," Mr. Hollinger admitted.

Upon hearing her favorite word, Sapphie leapt up and barked.

"I guess they weren't sleeping after all," Adam said. "You guys want to go for a walk?"

Corgi Capers: Deceit on Dorset Drive

"I'll go with you," Courtney said. "As long as you promise not to wear that dumb hat." She flicked Adam's detective hat onto the floor.

Adam rolled his eyes and opened the crates. "Courtney," he said, "you didn't latch Sapphie's crate all the way."

"Yes, I did."

"No, you didn't. It was nearly un-latched. Sapphie could have gotten loose."

"Whatever," Courtney smirked.

While Adam and Courtney dug through the pet shop bags to find leashes and collars, Sapphie turned quietly to Zeph. "Three? I mean, Zeph? What's a walk?"

Zeph shook his head. "I have no idea." The two puppies sat with their heads cocked in confusion as Adam and Courtney called their names and held out something strange, something Adam called a "collar."

~ SIXTEEN ~
A Suspicious Garage

Adam and Courtney had a tough time getting the puppies to stay still long enough to put their collars on. Zeph cried and cried, pressing himself firmly against the kitchen floor. He had never seen anything as scary as a collar, and he wasn't taking any chances!

But finally, with some calming words, Adam, put the collar on. Zeph froze for a minute, trembling a little, before realizing there wasn't anything scary about a collar.

Sapphie, on the other hand, struggled and bit. She made wild crying sounds that reminded Adam of a cat rather than a dog. She chewed at the collar, and even nipped at Courtney's hand.

"I can't do it," Courtney cried. "Maybe you can."

Adam shook his head. "Sapphie's too wild. Maybe if we work together..."

Courtney nodded. "I'll distract her. You put on the collar."

She called Sapphie to her. The little puppy wagged her tail and jumped onto Courtney's lap.

"Okay," Adam whispered. "Keep her calm while I slip the collar on."

Courtney scratched her puppy behind the ears, and Sapphie stared right into Courtney's eyes.

Corgi Capers: Deceit on Dorset Drive

"Do you like your name?" Courtney asked. "You're a princess, you know. Princess Sapphie."

The attention thrilled Sapphie, and before long Adam had quietly slipped the collar around her neck. But when she realized what had happened, Sapphie went crazy, barking, biting, and jumping. She ran in circles, trying to chase her collar away.

"Maybe the old woman at the pet shop was right," Adam said over the puppy's squeals.

Sapphie gave Adam an indignant look before Courtney picked her up and carried her outdoors.

Adam started to follow with Zeph in his arms, but he turned back, retrieved his detective hat, and hurried out the door, hoping once again that the hat might inspire him to solve the crime.

Outside, the puppies had a tough time adjusting to walking on a leash. They pulled in all directions, and when the leash went taut, they cried and jumped and bit. Sapphie growled in agitation, and Zeph cried in fear and threw himself onto the ground.

Down the street, the Davenports, who had been working in their garage, stopped to watch.

Sapphie grabbed hold of her leash and pulled with all her might toward the Davenports' garage.

"New puppies?" Mr. Davenport asked.

"Yes." Adam struggled to steady Zeph.

"Is this the first time they've been on a leash?"

"Yes! They've lived on a farm their whole lives. I doubt they've ever even *seen* a leash before."

Sapphie continued to growl and bite her leash, so Courtney finally picked her up.

"Sapphie will *never* learn to walk," she groaned.

"I have something in here that may help." Mrs. Davenport disappeared into her garage.

Zeph ran to follow. Adam wasn't expecting it, and he dropped the leash.

"You've gotta hold tight, Stupid," Courtney sneered.

But it was too late: Zeph was lost among the catacombs of the Davenports' garage. Parking a car in it would be out of the question. In fact, it reminded Adam of his father's junk room.

"You sure got a lot of stuff," Adam said to Mr. Davenport as he crouched down to locate Zeph.

"eBay," he explained.

"eBay?"

"We have an online business. We find stuff cheap, then sell it online for a profit."

"I see." Adam adjusted his detective hat. "Where do you get the stuff to sell?"

Corgi Capers: Deceit on Dorset Drive

But before Mr. Davenport could answer, Mrs. Davenport emerged from behind the stacks of boxes.

"Here, kids. I knew we had some extra dog harnesses in here. Why don't you try finding a size that fits? You know how they work?"

Mrs. Davenport placed a box of dog harnesses on the floor of the garage. Zeph emerged from behind a box and sniffed the harnesses suspiciously.

Adam grabbed Zeph's leash and then dug through the box. He found a red harness that seemed just a bit big on Zeph.

"They're adjustable," Mrs. Davenport said. "And of course your puppies will continue to grow..."

Despite the puppy's struggles, Adam managed to put a harness on Zeph and walked him up and down the driveway. With the new harness, Zeph didn't fidget at all. When the leash went taut, Zeph stopped and looked at Adam.

"It's like magic!" cried Adam. "How much do we owe you?" he asked as Courtney tried to put a pink harness on the squirming Sapphie.

"Oh, no charge for you. You're such good neighbors and all..."

"Thanks again," said Adam.

"Well, we'll let you get back to your walk," Mr. Davenport said.

"And be careful of the serial burglar," Courtney added. "He's struck again."

Corgi Capers: Deceit on Dorset Drive

"I know," Mr. Davenport said. "I'm sorry to hear about your home."

Adam turned around. "How do you know already?"

Mr. Davenport turned to his wife. She shrugged. "Um," he muttered. "I guess news just travels fast in this neighborhood."

When Adam and Courtney were well out of earshot, Adam turned to his sister.

"Did you notice anything fishy about what just happened?"

"What do you mean?" Courtney asked.

"I mean, Mister Davenport didn't answer where he got all his stuff to sell on eBay. And how could they possibly have heard about the burglaries?"

"Maybe they saw the police come to the house. Maybe Dad told them while we were at the pet shop. Don't be so suspicious."

"But their garage is *packed* with stuff. Maybe they're the burglars. A criminal couple like Bonnie and Clyde. Maybe they rob their neighbors and sell the stolen goods for profit."

"Bonnie and *who*? You're being paranoid. Besides, I didn't see any of our stuff in their garage, did you?" Courtney turned around to take another look at the garage.

"Though I guess you *could* be right."

"So you believe me?"

"Well, they *did* give us these free harnesses. Why would they do that?"

Corgi Capers: Deceit on Dorset Drive

"I don't know. Maybe they were just being neighborly."

"Maybe," Courtney replied. "Or maybe they feel guilty about robbing our house. It's the least they could do to make it up to us. Maybe they're thinking about all the money they're going to make by selling our stuff."

"Should we tell Mom and Dad?"

"Would they believe us?"

"It's hard to tell." Adam took off his hat and ran his fingers through his hair. He wondered what Riley Couth would do.

Before he could decide, Courtney's cell phone buzzed. She looked at its glowing screen.

"It's a text from Mom. She said we have to come home to help with the paperwork. She wants it done before we go to bed."

"Paperwork?"

"For the insurance company," Courtney groaned.

The two walked home in the setting sun. They were unhappy about the mess that awaited, but they were relieved, at least, that even Sapphie walked well with her new harness.

~ * ~

At home, Mr. Hollinger stood in the family room with a clipboard while Mrs. Hollinger hunched over the remains of the family's DVD collection.

Corgi Capers: Deceit on Dorset Drive

"Did we have a copy of *Ghostbusters*?" she asked.

"Yes," Mr. Hollinger said. "Your brother got it for us."

"Well it's missing now. Better mark it down."

Mr. Hollinger nodded and scribbled something on the clipboard.

"Don't forget," she added. "There's no apostrophe in the title."

Mr. Hollinger checked his grammar while Adam and Courtney entered with the puppies.

"Kids," he said. "We need you to go upstairs and write down anything that's missing from your rooms. Here, take this form."

He handed it to Adam.

"And write neatly," Mrs. Hollinger added.

"But nothing was touched in my room," Adam said.

"Then help Courtney, okay?"

Courtney huffed. "I don't want his grubby hands on my stuff!"

"Courtney!" Mr. Hollinger used his serious voice, and Courtney knew better than to push him.

"It's bad enough we didn't make a record of our belongings *before* the burglary. The last thing I need is for you two to start fighting."

"What about the puppies?" Adam asked, trying to change the subject. "Can they come upstairs with us?"

"Honey," Mrs. Hollinger said. "Puppies require a lot of supervision." She squinted at Sapphie. "They're not housebroken yet, and we have so much to do — we just can't worry about them messing on the carpet right now."

"But I don't want to put Sapphie in her crate." Courtney pouted. "It's too early for bed. Can't she stay in my room with me?"

"No," Mrs. Hollinger said firmly. "I need you to focus on listing exactly what's missing. It's important that you concentrate. Besides, puppies are growing creatures. They need even more sleep than you do."

Courtney huffed. "I don't want to put her in her crate yet." She turned to Adam. "Help me out."

"What about the child safety gate?" Adam asked. "The one Mom and Dad used to put on the stairs when we were little."

"What about it?" Mr. Hollinger asked. "It wasn't stolen. It's in the basement. The burglar didn't even go down there. Luckily."

"What if we used the safety gate to block off the door to the kitchen? Then we could leave the puppies in the kitchen. It's a vinyl floor, so it's easy to clean if they have an accident. And that way they don't have to stay in their crates just quite yet." He smiled at Courtney.

Corgi Capers: Deceit on Dorset Drive

"That's fine," Mr. Hollinger said, hurrying back to work.

"Just put them in their crates before you go to bed," Mrs. Hollinger added. "We don't want them running around the kitchen at all hours of the night."

Sapphie's eyes popped open at the idea of running around the kitchen. She barked once at Zeph to see if he had the same idea, but Zeph stared into space, lost in thought.

While Adam put the safety gate in the kitchen, Courtney got herself a drink of ice water from the freezer dispenser. She liked to listen to the ice cubes plop-plop-plop into her glass.

"You should put the ice cubes in the glass first," Adam said, "and *then* the water."

"Shut up. You're such a nerd!"

"Am not!"

Courtney giggled. "Just wait until Marnie Ellison shows all the kids in your class the picture of you with your pants wet."

"That was your stupid dog that peed on me," Adam said. "It's so unfair."

"That's what you get for being a stupid fifth grader." Courtney wasn't paying attention, and the ice cubes overfilled the glass. They tumbled onto the floor in a messy puddle of water.

The puppies were ecstatic. With their paws, they batted the ice cubes like hockey pucks. They barked and wagged, wagged and

Corgi Capers: Deceit on Dorset Drive

barked as they chased the ice around the kitchen.

"Isn't that cute?" Courtney asked, putting aside her disgust of her brother.

"It is," Adam agreed. "Where's your video camera? Let's film them."

"It's…" Courtney paused. "It *was* in my dresser. It's probably not there anymore."

The two lowered their eyes as they remembered the purple video camera their grandmother had gotten Courtney as a gift for entering middle school. They had been so happy to have it. They used to spend hours making movies together.

Now it was gone.

On that somber note, the siblings trudged up the stairs to spend the rest of the night making a list of all that was missing.

~ SEVENTEEN ~
Sorting Out Their New Home

As soon as Sapphie awoke the next morning, she started barking, waking Zeph up with a start.

"Three, where are we?" Sapphie asked frantically from her crate. Before Zeph could answer, she howled and whined and chased her tail around in fast circles.

"Sapphie, calm down." He remembered Owl's words and knew he had to look after his sister. "You're in your crate."

"My what?"

"Your Little House."

"Three!" she cried. "Where's One? Where's Two?"

"Calm down. I'm Zeph now, remember? We've left Pickwick farm. We're at our new home."

Sapphie froze and cocked her head for a moment. Then she howled.

"Sapphie," Zeph said, trying a different approach. "Maybe the woman at the pet store was right."

"Huh?" Sapphie whispered.

"She said you were off-balance."

"What are you talking about?"

Zeph pointed to the window with his nose. "Look outside," he said.

"Why?"

"It's still dark."

Corgi Capers: Deceit on Dorset Drive

"So?"

"So that means it's not time to wake up yet."

"But I'm not tired. I want to wake up now. Now, now, *now!*" Sapphie howled again.

"Sapphie, think back to the farm. Remember that time the four of us wanted to wake up in the middle of the night? We started running around the kitchen. You even got into the pantry. Do you remember that?"

Sapphie panted. "That was fun! Remember I knocked over a box of crackers, and we all ate them before our People came down to stop us? Why don't we try that now?" Sapphie shifted her body so that her front paw was level with the latch of her crate. "How did you say to open the crate again?"

"Sapphie, no," Zeph barked, forgetting to keep his voice down. "You can't escape now."

"Why not?"

"If you escape now, you'll wake your Person. If they know you can escape, they'll fix it so that it's impossible for you to get out ever again."

"No they won't."

"Yes they will," Zeph insisted. "Ma and Pa told us that. We're only supposed to escape from our crates if it's an emergency."

"Hmph! We'll *I'm* hungry, and that's an emergency if I ever heard one! I don't even understand how I got in here." She bit the edge of her crate. "I thought we were going

Corgi Capers: Deceit on Dorset Drive

to run around the kitchen all night."

"Think, Sapphie. Last night our People came into the kitchen and told us it was time for bed. Remember?"

"No."

"You ran in circles around your Person. It took her twelve tries to catch you."

"Oh, *that* I remember! That was fun. Let's escape and do it again."

Zeph growled. "We can't just escape whenever we feel like it. We have to save our escape for when it's needed most — an emergency. Besides, Sapphie, you didn't let me finish what I was saying. That night we all started running wild in the pantry. Do you remember what happened?"

"Ma started barking, I remember," she said.

"After that."

"After that, just as the sun was coming up, I curled up and went to sleep."

"Before that," Zeph said, trying to stay patient.

"Hmmm. I don't remember."

"Grandpa Pickwick came downstairs, all groggy with sleep, and he yelled for us to be quiet. Do you remember what he had in his hand?"

"A cookie?"

"Of course not. We were in trouble! He had that Scary Can."

Zeph thought back to that terrible night. Grandpa Pickwick held up an ordinary-looking tin can. But when he shook it, it made such a loud, jingling clatter that all four puppies immediately ran to the protection of their parents. After Grandpa Pickwick returned upstairs, the puppies couldn't fall asleep for hours. They didn't understand that it was only Grandpa Pickwick's coin jar.

Sapphie yelped at the memory. Her ears darted back. "That was scary!"

"Well, if you keep barking, or if you escape from your crate, our new People might come down with a Scary Can of their own."

"I don't want that."

"Then go back to sleep."

Sapphie nodded. "Are you going to sleep, too?"

"No," Zeph growled.

"Why not?"

"There's something strange going on around here, and I need time to figure out what it is. There's a lot of new smells and a lot of new people. I'm trying to sort it out."

"Want me to help?" asked Sapphie, jumping up against the door of her crate.

"No. The best thing you can do to help me think is to go back to sleep."

Zeph stared out the window watching the pink sun peek above the horizon. Sapphie settled in, and soon her breath became steady with sleep. And there, in the still of the morning, Zeph stared out the window until he was lost in thought.

~ EIGHTEEN ~
A Devastating Disaster

In the morning, the family sat down to a somber breakfast. Mrs. Hollinger kept talking about some sentimental jewelry that was taken. Mr. Hollinger complained about having to tell his clients about their personal information being stolen.

Courtney was disgusted that her room had been rummaged. "Even my underwear drawer. Gross!" she moaned.

Courtney hated when *anyone* looked in her room, let alone a complete stranger.

Adam, who had only lost a handful of video games, felt lucky. They could be easily replaced and held no sentimental value. As the family brooded at the breakfast table, Adam played with the puppies. Sapphie played fetch with the squirrel squeak toy. Zeph, who didn't quite understand the concept of "fetch," was content just chasing his sister around the kitchen.

"The gate works pretty good," Adam said to his family. "It keeps the dogs in the kitchen where they can play without getting into trouble."

"Pretty *well*," Mrs. Hollinger added half-heartedly. "At least the kitchen floor is easy to clean. Sapphie's going to be a challenge to housebreak."

Mr. Hollinger groaned and slurped the

Corgi Capers: Deceit on Dorset Drive

rest of his coffee. "I've got to run to the hardware store. I'm going to fix the broken window and the living room drawer. Anyone coming?"

The room was silent. No one seemed to want to do anything — except Adam.

"I'll come," Adam said.

"I've got too much to clean," Mrs. Hollinger said.

Mr. Hollinger nodded. "Courtney, you watch the dogs. We'll all have to pitch in today."

Adam watched his dad out of the corner of his eye. He'd never heard his father sound so bitter about anything before. Mrs. Hollinger averted her eyes and picked at her napkin. Even Courtney didn't complain about being told to watch the dogs.

The atmosphere of the house was tense, and Adam was glad for the trip to the hardware store. But even as Mr. Hollinger drove, he didn't say a word.

"Hey, Dad," Adam said, trying to break the silence. "Did Mom tell you about Autumn League?"

"No." Mr. Hollinger stared at the road blankly for a moment. Then Adam's words seemed to snap him out of his bad mood. "What about Autumn League?"

"Well, the bad news is that Bryce broke his arm the other day."

"Isn't he the star pitcher? The one who strikes out almost everyone?"

Corgi Capers: Deceit on Dorset Drive

"Yeah. He was our secret weapon. We'll have to play without him. But that's the good news. Coach let me try pitching yesterday, and I was pretty good."

"Oh yeah?" Mr. Hollinger's eyes lit up. "I always knew you should be doing more than just outfield." He smiled and seemed to forget all about his problems for the moment.

"Well, don't get carried away. We're having official try-outs for pitcher next practice."

"We'll have to practice later," Mr. Hollinger said. "I could use a break from all this burglary nonsense. It's gotten me in such a bad mood."

At the hardware store, Mr. Hollinger searched through the aisles for the supplies he'd need to make repairs. In the meantime, Adam found a dog tag machine at the front of the store. For two dollars, the machine created a dog tag engraved with the dog's name and family contact information. For four dollars, Adam could choose a customized shape. Adam liked the round blue one. He inserted a five-dollar bill he had earned weeding Mrs. Pinkney's gardens and engraved a tag for Zeph.

He tucked the tag safely in his wallet and started down the aisle to find his father, but something tugged at him. As annoying as Courtney was, she would probably like a tag for Sapphie. Besides, if either of the pups were to break loose and get lost, it would

Corgi Capers: Deceit on Dorset Drive

probably be Sapphie.

He reached into his wallet for the only other money he had with him: a five-dollar bill he'd earned for watering a neighbor's tomato plants while they were on vacation. He stuck it in the machine and picked a pink heart for Sapphie. He hoped Courtney would like it. Maybe it would make her feel better after having her room ransacked.

When he showed Courtney the dog tag later at home, she actually smiled and thanked him. They put the tags on the puppies' collars and smiled together as Sapphie and Zeph ran around the kitchen, howling at the way the new tags clanged and clanked on their collars. It was a moment of peace with Courtney.

But the peace didn't last long.

"Courtney!" Mrs. Hollinger called down the stairs.

Courtney rolled her eyes. "Yeah, Mom?"

"I need you to come up here and help me vacuum."

"Do I have to?"

"Right now, Courtney!" Mrs. Hollinger yelled.

"What's wrong with Mom?" Adam whispered. "She's never this mad, and she's never this obsessed with cleaning."

"She's mad because the burglar stole a necklace Dad gave her the day they met. It was a charm in the shape of a seashell on a silver chain."

"I remember that necklace."

Courtney nodded. "It was her favorite one, and now it's gone."

"That's sad," Adam said.

"The worst part is that it's put Mom in such a bad mood. It's like she's taking out all her frustrations on me." Then, Courtney yelled up the stairs. "Adam's home too, you know!"

"Well I'll need his help, too. I need you both to do some vacuuming. And I need you to clean out the minivan. I think we all left some supplies and shopping bags in it last night after all the craziness."

Courtney stuck her tongue out at Adam. It was as if she'd already forgotten about the dog tag.

"I'll vacuum first," she said. "Do something useful and watch the dogs, will ya?"

Adam rolled his eyes and wondered if Courtney would ever lose her attitude. He sat down on the kitchen floor, and Zeph ran to him, resting his nose on Adam's leg.

"Good boy."

Zeph rolled onto his back, happy to have all of Adam's attention.

But Sapphie didn't like it one bit. *She* was supposed to have all the attention! She took a running leap into Adam's lap, distracting him from petting Zeph. She kicked and squirmed until she pushed Zeph out of the way. She squealed happily, glad to have stolen the spotlight.

"Alright, Sapphie," Adam said. "Want to play fetch?" He squeaked the squirrel toy and threw it across the kitchen. Distracted, Sapphie chased it, her new tag jingling. While she was distracted, Zeph inched his way back to Adam's lap.

Before long, Sapphie plopped down next to Adam. She panted, and her tongue dripped onto the kitchen floor. "I'm going to have to go help upstairs," Adam said.

He stood to leave, but both dogs whined.

"I wish I could stay," he said. "I wish Mom weren't in such a bad mood. I wish I could find everyone's stolen items and figure out who the burglar is. But I can't. I wonder how Riley Couth would handle this situation."

He looked down at the puppies. They whined.

"I'll bet you guys would like something soft to snuggle up on while you're in the kitchen." Both puppies dropped to the floor and sat at attention, tails wagging.

"Would you like that?" Each puppy cocked its head. Zeph let out a little bark.

"Okay. I'll go get our old comforter."

He stepped over the safety gate and crept downstairs all the way into the basement where the Hollingers kept their old blankets. He had one in mind: a very old comforter with blue flowers. The Hollingers some-

Corgi Capers: Deceit on Dorset Drive

times used it as a picnic blanket for Independence Day fireworks.

Adam turned on the single light bulb at the bottom of the stairs. The basement was always creepy: the shadows from the light bulb, the growling furnace, the unfinished cinderblock walls. Adam shivered.

In the corner was a set of shelves and an old chair. On top of the chair, Adam saw the comforter he was looking for. But as he reached to grab it, something caught his eye. On the shelves were some old photo albums his parents had from before Adam or Courtney was born.

The one he reached for was a shiny white wedding album. On the cover was a picture of Adam's parents. They looked so young. His mom's hair was so long; it practically touched her waist. And his dad had a beard!

Adam laughed.

He opened the book, squinting in the dim light as he flipped through the album. There was a picture of Grandma there. She looked more different than anyone. Her hair, now completely white, was dark brown and super short. Adam could hardly believe it.

A barking puppy upstairs made Adam pause. *"I should really get back to the puppies,"* he thought. He promised himself just one more page. That was when he saw it: a picture of the iridescent seashell necklace. It was a photo of Mrs. Hollinger in close-up. Someone had scrawled a caption at the bot-

Corgi Capers: Deceit on Dorset Drive

tom of the picture: *when we met*. The seashell was pale and shiny blue. In the picture,
Mrs. Hollinger had such a smile on her face.

Adam felt terrible that his mother's
necklace had been stolen. It probably wasn't
worth all that much money, but it meant so
much to his mother. He took the photo as evidence, thinking it would be something Riley
Couth might do.

As he carefully put the photo album
away, he tried to think of a way to catch the
burglar. What if it *was* the Davenports? What
if they were running their online business by
selling stolen merchandise? Adam vowed to
find out.

On his way upstairs, he grabbed his
gray detective hat from the coat rack, eager
to solve the crime. He stuck the photo of the
necklace inside the hat's lining and popped
the hat on his head.

As he passed his mother, he heard the
skittering of the puppies across the kitchen
floor, and also something that didn't sound
quite right — the faint sound of paper tearing.
But his mother's words distracted him from
investigating.

"Oh, Adam, I was calling for you. I
guess you didn't hear me."

"I was looking for this comforter. Is it
okay if the dogs use it?"

"Sure. It's old as anything. Anyway, I
got your friend's comic book from the
minivan. I told Courtney to bring it to you. Did

Corgi Capers: Deceit on Dorset Drive

you get it?"

"No."

"Courtney," Mrs. Hollinger yelled up the stairs. "Where did you put Adam's comic book?"

"It's on the kitchen table," Courtney yelled back.

Adam filled with a sense of dread. Suddenly, he knew what was making the sound — and it made him feel very sick. He walked to the kitchen slowly, stepping over the child gate. To his horror, the table was empty. He looked down at the kitchen floor. It was littered with torn scraps of Patrick's comic book. Here, Logan Zephyr's face. There, Princess Sapphire's foot.

"Patrick will never forgive me," Adam muttered. "Mom!" he screamed.

But Mrs. Hollinger was already on her way to the garage to find cleaning supplies.

Sapphie ran across the floor holding a picture of a spaceship in her mouth. Zeph was content to roll on his back all over the torn paper.

Adam looked at the puppies. He was mad, but he knew it wasn't their fault. "Bad dogs," he started to say, but their eyes looked so sad. How were they supposed to know what a comic book was? He placed the comforter on the ground and stormed upstairs. He knew whose fault it was, really.

"Courtney!" he screamed, barging into her room.

Corgi Capers: Deceit on Dorset Drive

"You idiot!" Her face turned bright red. "No one enters my room without knocking first!"

"But the door was open."

"It doesn't matter. It's *my* room!"

The room was still disheveled, and Adam looked at Courtney's clipboard. There was a fairly long list of missing items. It must have put Courtney in a very bad mood.

"The dogs destroyed Patrick's comic book. It wasn't on the table. It was on the floor."

"Well I tossed it on the table."

"Are you sure it landed there?"

"Yes!" She paused. "Maybe."

"Maybe? Courtney, that was a limited-edition comic book. Patrick's going to be so mad. Why did you toss it?"

"I didn't feel like stepping over the safety gate."

"That's dumb."

"Not as dumb as you! It's just a stupid comic book."

"It's a limited edition Logan Zephyr series! And it's Patrick's! You've got bad aim. You should have made sure it landed on the table."

Courtney shrugged. "I've got better aim than you. You're just an outfielder."

Adam had to fight the urge to punch his sister.

"What am I supposed to tell Patrick?"

"Tell him it got stolen when our house

Corgi Capers: Deceit on Dorset Drive

was broken into."

"That's a lie."

"So?"

"It wouldn't feel right."

"What a nerd."

"You should pay for it."

"Yeah, right. Even if I *did* have money, there's no way you're getting any of it. Why don't you check eBay or something? Or maybe see if the Davenports have a copy to sell you." She laughed, then pushed her brother into the hallway and slammed the door just as her mother was coming up the stairs with the vacuum cleaner.

"What's going on?" Mrs. Hollinger asked.

"Courtney threw my comic book in the kitchen, and it landed on the floor, and the dogs chewed it up, and it belongs to Patrick, and it's a limited edition, and now Patrick's going to kill me!"

"Settle down. You two need to work this out. I really don't have time to deal with you and your sister fighting...with all the in-surance paperwork and phone calls to the po-lice..."

Adam opened his mouth to tell his mother about the Davenports, but he decided at the last minute it would be a bad idea.

"Besides," Mrs. Hollinger said. "It's your turn to vacuum. I need you to do the se-cond floor."

"Fine. I guess I'll have to vacuum up

Corgi Capers: Deceit on Dorset Drive

the ruins of the comic book from the kitchen, too."

Adam wanted to say more, but the look on his mother's face made him hurry away without another word.

~ NINETEEN ~
What's in a Name?

While Adam was upstairs, Zeph and Sapphie finished tearing apart the comic book.

"That was fun," said Sapphie, sitting on a pile of scraps. "It was nice of Courtney to give us such a fun toy."

"I don't know," Zeph said, plopping down on the old comforter. "When Adam came in here, he seemed upset."

"You worry too much," Sapphie said, and pounced on her brother. She wrestled him until she was out of breath. Then she asked, "Zeph, what does 'Princess' mean?"

Zeph growled at her.

"You don't *know*?" she teased. "I thought you knew *every word that existed!*"

Zeph paused for a moment, considering his answer. As the smartest of the four corgi siblings, he paid very close attention to the words people said. He understood spoken language very well. Of course he knew what 'princess' meant.

"I do know," he said slowly. "I just don't know if I should tell you."

"Why not?" Sapphie yelped and wagged her tail.

"Because, it might go to your head."

Sapphie couldn't take the suspense any

Corgi Capers: Deceit on Dorset Drive

longer. She jumped up and down. "Tell me, tell me, *tell me!*" she barked.

Before Zeph could respond, Courtney came into the room for a drink of water.

She sneered at the puppies. "You two got me in trouble with Adam. You shouldn't have chewed that comic book...even if it *is* nerdy."

Sapphie ran to Courtney, her little tail wagging so hard her entire body swung from side to side. Zeph, however, hung his head. He understood enough of what Courtney said to know he'd been bad.

Still mad, Courtney ignored them and got a drink from the refrigerator. But as she looked down, she thought about how she should have been more careful with her brother's comic book. She pressed the ice cube dispenser and listened to the ice plop-plop-plop into her drink.

Zeph let out a soft howl just like Owl.

"Want ice?" Courtney asked.

Both dogs stiffened. Their legs tensed, ready to pounce. Courtney couldn't help but smile.

"Here!" She let two ice cubes fall from the machine. They clanked onto the floor, and the two dogs went wild chasing them all over the kitchen.

"I'll be back if I ever finish cleaning," she said before climbing over the safety gate.

In the meantime, Zeph sat on the comforter eating his ice cube. Sapphie joined him, but she preferred to lick her cube slowly, making a cold, wet mess on the comforter.

"Our People will think you had an accident there," Zeph warned. "You should just crunch on the ice cube like I'm doing. You haven't been doing so well on your housetraining."

"I prefer my way," Sapphie said indignantly. Then she remembered: "You never told me what 'princess' means!"

"Why do you care so much?"

"Because I heard Courtney say that my real name isn't just Sapphie. It's *Princess* Sapphie."

Zeph growled again.

"Why won't you tell me?"

"I don't want it to go to your head."

"What's wrong with my head?" Sapphie jumped up on her brother, biting his ear.

He yelped. "That hurts!"

"Tell me what it means, and I'll stop."

"No."

"Fine!" Sapphie let go of his ear and backed up. Then, she took a running leap, pouncing on Zeph and knocking him to the ground. She jumped on top of him and bit at his throat playfully — but not very gently. She had no intention of stopping until she had her answer.

"Fine," Zeph yelped again. "Just stop biting. It hurts."

Sapphie let him go and sat at attention, her little tail wagging furiously. "What does it

Corgi Capers: Deceit on Dorset Drive

mean? What does it mean?"

Zeph sat up slowly, straightening himself out. "That hurt, you know. You shouldn't do that to me."

"Hmph!" Sapphie said.

Zeph shook himself off and spoke slowly. "The word 'princess' means royalty. A princess is someone who has power. A princess is someone other people have to obey."

Sapphie's eyes lit up. Her entire body wagged. "And *I'm* a *princess*! Does that mean I'm in charge here? That People have to serve me? That even *you* have to serve me?"

"But a princess also has a great responsibility," Zeph added.

But his sister was no longer listening. She was too busy running around the kitchen crying, "Princess, princess, *princess*!"

She turned and wagged her tail right in Zeph's face. Then she took all of her chew toys — and his as well — and sat on the comforter, chewing on them daintily.

Zeph sighed. He'd have to deal with his sister later. But there was a more pressing issue at the moment. Something didn't quite seem right, and Zeph vowed to find out what it was. He sat down on the shredded remains of the comic book and thought to himself that he needed very much to find Adam.

~ TWENTY ~
Open Doors

In the kitchen, Adam plugged in the vacuum and turned it on. The noise sent Sapphie into a barking frenzy. She charged at the vacuum, snapping her teeth at the long hose. Zeph barked and ran into his crate, trembling. Adam turned off the machine.

"It's just a vacuum," he said.

Zeph crept out of his crate slowly, sniffing at the machine.

Sapphie ran in circles around it.

"See?" Adam said. "It's okay."

He turned the vacuum on again, and Sapphie went on the offensive, attacking the vacuum. Zeph ran back into his crate.

Once more, Adam turned off the vacuum. "Courtney," he yelled up the stairs. "Can you watch the puppies while I vacuum the kitchen?"

"Bring them up here."

Adam rolled his eyes. "What a princess," he mumbled and gently picked up Sapphie, who turned with delight to look at her brother.

"*See?*" Her look seemed to say, "*I really am a princess.*"

Adam called "Here, boy," and Zeph followed.

"Can you get up the stairs?" Adam asked his puppy. He pointed to the stairs

Corgi Capers: Deceit on Dorset Drive

leading to the bedrooms. "Go find Courtney."

Adam placed Sapphie at the foot of the stairs. With a sharp yelp, she sprinted up, moving quickly for a dog with such short legs. She had learned to climb stairs back on Pickwick Farm, where she often snuck up to the second-floor bedrooms when no one else was looking.

Zeph had never snuck up a staircase before. He watched his sister and cried. He didn't seem to understand what to do.

"Here." Adam placed Zeph's front two paws on the first step, then lifted his back two paws to follow. He did this for the next three steps. Finally, Zeph understood and made it up the rest of the flight on his own.

Adam patted both puppies when they reached the top. Then he knocked on Courtney's door.

"Here are the puppies," he said.

Courtney was reclining on the bed reading a magazine. She hardly looked up.

Adam shook his head. "You could have gotten them yourself."

"Mom just made me vacuum the whole upstairs. I'm tired. And I'm working on my list of what was stolen."

"You don't look like you're working."

Courtney looked guiltily at her fashion magazine. "I just vacuumed a lot. I need a break. I'll start working again in, like, five minutes."

As small as she was, Sapphie took a

running leap and curled up at the foot of Courtney's bed. Zeph sat on the floor below, howling at his sister above.

Adam shook his head and glanced around. The hallway looked somewhat vacuumed, and Courtney's room did, too. His bedroom had not been vacuumed at all.

The junk room door, normally securely shut, was wide open. It was clear that Courtney had tried her best to vacuum around all the clutter.

Mr. Hollinger kept a "pathway" cleared from the door to the chair, from the chair to the bookshelves, and from the bookshelves to the stack of newspapers. It made Adam laugh sometimes at how messy it was, but it also made him mad. It didn't seem fair that he and Courtney had to keep their rooms neat while their father got to keep his junk room as messy as he liked.

"Remember to watch them. You don't want them to have an accident on your carpet," Adam reminded Courtney.

He closed her bedroom door so the puppies couldn't get loose and returned to the kitchen.

Down on the second floor, Adam finished cleaning up the scraps of Patrick's comic book. Then, with his detective hat on, he vacuumed the living room and dining room. He tried to look for clues the burglar might have left behind, but all he found were scattered possessions that belonged to his family.

Corgi Capers: Deceit on Dorset Drive

When he had finished, he put the vacuum cleaner back in the garage and went upstairs to get the puppies. He was sure to knock before entering.

"What do you want?" Courtney asked.

"I came to take the puppies back to the kitchen."

"Good. They're hard to watch. They like to chew everything."

Adam opened the door. Sapphie was sitting on Courtney's bed — right on Courtney's pillow — and Courtney was rubbing her with her toe as she flipped through her magazine. Zeph was sitting on the floor chewing on a pencil.

"Zeph!" Adam called.

"Oh, let him chew it. It's only a stupid pencil. Not like I'll ever use it."

"You could have gotten him a chew toy or something. Pencils aren't good for him."

"Whatever. Leave me alone. I'm trying to finish reading." She pointed to her glossy magazine. "If you want the dogs, take them."

"Come on," Adam called. "We'll go back to the kitchen."

Zeph jumped up immediately, his tail wagging. Sapphie raised her head, looked at Adam briefly, then lowered her head again and snuggled onto the pillow.

"Fine. I'll take Zeph downstairs. Don't forget about Sapphie."

"You think I'm stupid? I'm the one in middle school."

Corgi Capers: Deceit on Dorset Drive

Adam left as quickly as possible.

"Close my door," Courtney yelled down the hallway, but Adam was already carrying Zeph down the stairs. Courtney, very comfortably lounging on her bed, decided she would leave it open, at least for now.

A few minutes later, Sapphie started fidgeting. Where was Zeph? When was he coming back? She tried to nuzzle with Courtney, but Courtney pushed her away.

"You're sitting on top of my magazine!" she scolded. "Here, sit on the floor."

Courtney lifted Sapphie onto the floor, placing her on a nice smelly pile of laundry in the corner. Sapphie found a particularly soft sweatshirt, wagged her tail and circled three times before settling in. Every time Courtney moved, Sapphie's eyes opened, and she gave a little bark.

Then Courtney would say, "It's okay, Sapphie," and the puppy would settle back into place, close her eyes again, and doze off to sleep.

At one point, a particularly strange ringing woke Sapphie. She barked softly and lifted her head, waiting for Courtney to tell her everything was okay. But Courtney didn't seem to hear the bark. Instead, she was playing with a sparkly pink and purple toy with lots of shiny, glowing buttons.

"Hello? Aileen?" Courtney was saying.

But she wasn't speaking to Sapphie this time: she was speaking to her sparkly toy.

~ TWENTY-ONE ~
Sapphie's Adventure

Courtney was paying so much attention to her sparkly little toy that Sapphie easily snuck out of the bedroom. She sniffed around the hallway looking for something interesting to play with. At one end of the hallway were stairs. Stairs were such fun! She went up and down, down and up. Finally, when she was tired of that, she ran back upstairs.

She crept past Courtney's open door, but Courtney was too busy talking to notice her. She peeked into Mrs. Hollinger's room, but Mrs. Hollinger was too busy looking at a piece of paper and talking quietly to herself. Besides, the bedroom was *very* tidy. How boring!

Sapphie continued down the hall until she reached the junk room. What a room! It was full of fun things to smell. She sniffed around, going from one box to the next. She chewed a little bit on an old sock she found lodged behind the desk. Then she chewed on the corner of a cardboard box. But the most interesting thing she found was the stack of old newspapers. Nothing smelled quite the same as the inky newsprint.

The puppy hopped up on her two hind legs and tried to jump on top of the stack. It seemed like a fun thing to sit on — imagine all the things she'd be able to see from such a height! But after a few tries she saw it would be nearly impossible to climb. It was just too high.

Sapphie circled the stack just to make sure and found something very interesting sticking out of the back. It was a sports section from three months ago that had not been stacked straight. If she could read, she would have learned how a local high-school athlete hit the game-winning homerun with two outs at the bottom of the ninth. But she was much more interested in the paper's chewable qualities.

With a playful growl, she grasped the paper between her teeth and pulled as hard as she could. At first the pages didn't budge. But she tightened her grip and stood on her hind legs, giving herself more leverage. The pile shifted. She pulled and pulled until finally, the sports page came loose. But before she could sink her teeth into it, the whole stack shook and toppled right on top of her. She was stuck under the weight of the papers.

As she lay trapped, she remembered Zeph's warning about the importance of crates in keeping puppies out of trouble. Why hadn't she listened? She tried to move, but she was stuck. Whatever was on top of her was too heavy. Above, she saw a small opening.

"Help, help, *help!*" she cried, but her voice was muffled by the papers.

Corgi Capers: Deceit on Dorset Drive

Resolved to the situation, she did the only thing she could think of: she closed her eyes and fell into a fitful sleep.

In the meantime, Adam had taken Zeph to the first floor family room. He placed Zeph on his rocket ship bed and gave him a chew toy.

"You stay," he told the puppy. "I need to do some research."

Quietly, Adam logged onto the computer. He kept adjusting his detective hat as he searched eBay for the limited edition comic book. It was already sold out in most stores. The cheapest copy he could find was currently selling for 150 dollars, but the auction didn't end for another four days. At this rate, replacing Patrick's comic would use up all his savings.

Even though Adam had told Zeph to "stay," the puppy couldn't ignore the strange smell coming from the other end of the room where Mr. Hollinger had patched the broken window with a piece of plywood. Unable to help himself, Zeph crept out of his bed, his nose sniffing quickly.

Too upset to notice his puppy, Adam stared at the computer screen wondering what to do about Patrick's comic book. Before long he was thinking about the seashell necklace. "It's worth a shot," he told himself and searched for "blue seashell necklace." A handful of results came back — one that had

Corgi Capers: Deceit on Dorset Drive

been listed just this morning.

"Iridescent seashell necklace, used, good condition," he read aloud. "Bidding starts at twenty-five dollars."

He clicked on the "calculate shipping" button. It was shipping from Stoney Brook, his own hometown! And worst of all, the picture looked identical to the one Adam had seen in his mother's wedding album.

He pointed to the screen name: Snow-Town1877. "This has to be the thief," he said, but no one was around to hear.

Zeph, who had been sniffing near the broken window, was startled and ran back to the dog bed, curled up, and pretended he had been obedient the whole time.

Adam turned to Zeph. "Zeph, I found the thief!"

But Zeph was curled up not in his rocket bed, but in Sapphie's powder blue princess bed.

"Zeph!" Adam cried. "That's a girl's bed. No, Zeph. No!"

Zeph sat up.

Adam jumped to the floor and patted the rocket ship bed. "This is your bed. This is a *boy's* bed. You can't sleep in a princess bed, or everyone will think you're a 'fraidy cat!"

Zeph stretched, then moved to his rocket ship bed.

"Good boy," Adam said. "Now, Zeph, we need to think of a plan to catch the thief..."

Corgi Capers: Deceit on Dorset Drive

Just then, Courtney shrieked loudly enough for the whole house to hear. Zeph jumped up and ran up the flight of steps as quickly as he could. Adam took off his detective hat and followed.

"What's wrong?" Mrs. Hollinger was asking when Adam reached the third floor.

"Sapphie's gone! I don't know where she went," Courtney cried. "She was in my room. On that pile of clothes right there."

"Weren't you watching her?" Mrs. Hollinger asked. "She's only a puppy, you know."

"It's his fault." Courtney pointed at Adam, who now appeared in the doorway.

"How is it my fault?"

"You didn't close my door, Stupid. If you had listened to me and closed my door, Sapphie wouldn't have gotten out."

"It's not my fault you're lazy," Adam said.

"Kids. Kids!" Mrs. Hollinger yelled. "Now is not the time. Let's think about where Sapphie can be."

Adam was already down the hall. "She's not in my room," he called. "I checked under the bed, in the closet..."

"I've been in my bedroom the whole time," Mrs. Hollinger said. "I would have noticed her come in."

Just then, Zeph barked from down the hall.

"Zeph?" Adam followed the sound of the barking — right into Mr. Hollinger's junk

Corgi Capers: Deceit on Dorset Drive

room. "Maybe Zeph found her."

By now, Mr. Hollinger had come in from his office outside.

"I heard a scream. Is everyone okay?" His nerves were still on edge from the burglary.

"Sapphie's missing," Mrs. Hollinger explained.

"I think she's in your junk room," Adam said.

The family crowded around the junk room door. With Adam inside, there wasn't room for anyone else.

Meanwhile, Zeph barked softly, pawing at a cardboard box.

"Here, let me..." Mr. Hollinger said. Adam stepped into the hallway to make room for Mr. Hollinger. Like an expert, Mr. Hollinger stepped around his piles of newspapers, his boxes and stacks of junk.

"Looks like there's been a collapse," he explained.

"How can you tell?" Adam asked. "It looks like the same old mess to me."

Mr. Hollinger smiled, but he seemed embarrassed. "It may be messy, but it's my mess. I know it well. For example, all my old college stuff is in those boxes over there. The box beneath this stack has some high school memorabilia."

He stopped and looked at the expression on his son's face. "Of course that's neither here nor there. The point is, this newspaper pile right here." He pointed to the pile that covered Sapphie. "Isn't supposed to be a pile at all. It's supposed to be a nice, neat stack."

Zeph barked wildly.

"Easy, boy," Adam said.

"Oh, Doug!" Mrs. Hollinger cried. "Do you think Sapphie got trapped under the pile? Do you think she's okay?"

Courtney screamed and ran into her room, shutting the door. "I hate you, Adam. This is all your fault!"

"I didn't do anything."

"Quick, let's lift the papers," Mrs. Hollinger urged.

Slowly, gently, Mr. Hollinger lifted the papers, piece by piece. As he got toward the bottom, the newspapers started moving. Zeph barked happily, then jumped onto the stack, digging furiously to the bottom. When all the newspapers were gone, a dazed, sleepy puppy sat up, looking slowly around the room. Sapphie was safe.

Mr. Hollinger lifted the puppy carefully and examined her for injury.

"Thank goodness she's okay."

"Courtney!" everyone called.

When Courtney emerged from her room, she grabbed Sapphie and sniffled softly.

"Now that you know your puppy is safe, do you have anything you'd like to say?" asked Mrs. Hollinger.

Courtney frowned. "No."

Corgi Capers: Deceit on Dorset Drive

Mr. Hollinger cleared his throat. "Courtney…"

The look on his face told Courtney he wasn't kidding.

"Adam, I'm sorry I blamed you for not closing my door. I wasn't watching Sapphie while talking on the phone. There, I said it." Courtney looked away from her brother.

"Thanks," Adam muttered.

Courtney started to stomp off to her room again, when she turned back. "Dad, it's also not fair that you get to keep your junk room so messy. Sapphie could have been crushed if any of those boxes had fallen on her. If Adam and I have to keep our rooms clean, I think you should have to do something about this mess."

Mr. Hollinger rubbed his neck. His face turned red. He opened his mouth as if to speak, but it was too late: Courtney had stormed back to her room.

Mr. and Mrs. Hollinger and Adam looked at each other in an awkward silence. So many bad things had happened in the past twenty-four hours that no one quite knew what to say.

What's more, Adam remembered his discovery on eBay and contemplated telling his parents, but just as he was about to say something, Mrs. Hollinger spoke.

"Doug, your junk room *is* dangerous. You're a grown man. When are you going to

Corgi Capers: Deceit on Dorset Drive

learn to keep things neat?"

This annoyed Mr. Hollinger.

"When we moved here, you said you didn't mind if I kept the junk room to myself. The door is always supposed to be closed. If it had been closed, this never would have happened," Mr. Hollinger said.

He looked upset, and his reddish hair seemed to have more gray in it than normal.

"Don't try to blame others," Mrs. Hollinger warned. "You sound like Courtney."

"Susan, I'm not blaming anyone."

Adam could tell the conversation was escalating into a fight, and he didn't want any part of it. His parents were so stressed out from the burglary: it was clear they were just taking their anger out on each other.

So before things got any worse, he picked up Zeph and hurried back into the family room to continue his research.

Corgi Capers: Deceit on Dorset Drive

~ TWENTY-TWO ~
To Tell or Not to Tell

In the family room, Adam hunched over the computer, still searching for a replacement comic book. He didn't even hear when his father came down the steps.

"What's up, Adam?" Mr. Hollinger asked.

"Just looking for something," he muttered.

"Looking for what?"

"Courtney gave the dogs Patrick's limited-edition comic book, and they chewed it up. The cheapest one I can find is a hundred and fifty dollars. And it's an auction, so it might go up in price by the time the auction's over."

"Maybe Patrick doesn't need it back. Maybe he's already read it. Or maybe if you asked him, he'd let you replace it with a regular edition."

"No," Adam insisted. "He wants his special edition. Dad, this isn't just any comic. This is Logan Zephyr and the Stellar Squadron."

"I see," Mr. Hollinger said. "I remember when I was a kid. There was always that special comic book out there, the one everyone wanted. For me, it was a comic book about pirates..." His eyes wandered. "I'll bet I

Corgi Capers: Deceit on Dorset Drive

even have a copy somewhere in my junk room."

Adam cleared his throat.

"Well," Mr. Hollinger said, snapping out of his reverie. "I'll talk to Courtney later."

"Hmph." Adam crossed his arms. It seemed like Courtney never got in trouble, no matter what.

"How about practicing some pitching?" Mr. Hollinger asked.

Pitching! In all the excitement and dis-appointment of the past day, Adam complete-ly forgot about practicing his pitching. "Sure!"

As Adam turned off the computer, he wondered whether he should tell his dad about the eBay seller. He hadn't been able to find his dad's computer listed for sale, but he did find lots of other things, including a sea-shell necklace. But he knew his dad was most upset about his work computer. And what would he say if Adam accused the Davenports of the burglaries?

Adam couldn't decide what to do, so he put Zeph in the kitchen and followed his fa-ther outside to practice his pitching.

Mr. Hollinger waited in the street. Be-hind him rose Mr. Frostburg's house, high up on the hill — the same hill where the Stoys lived.

"If I miss, Mr. Frostburg's hill will stop the ball," Mr. Hollinger explained.

"As long as it doesn't land on the Stoys' yard," Adam muttered, sliding on his glove.

Corgi Capers: Deceit on Dorset Drive

"I'd hate for them to come out here and lecture us about property boundaries."

Adam's first few pitches lacked control, and one ball slammed right into Mr. Frostburg's steep hill. Adam could see a figure come to the window of his house, peer out at the lawn, then disappear from sight.

"Maybe we shouldn't play here," Adam said.

"What do you mean?"

"I saw Mr. Frostburg through his window. I don't think he likes it when the ball hits his lawn."

"I'm sure he doesn't mind. After all, he was a boy once, too."

"When? Like a million years ago?"

Mr. Hollinger couldn't help but smile. "Be nice. You'll get old too, one day."

"Not likely," Adam said, and threw another fastball right into Mr. Hollinger's glove.

"You're doing great," Mr. Hollinger said after a good long while. "You've really mastered the fastball. Now move your fingers over just slightly. Let's try for a slider."

Adam tried and tried, and finally he got one right.

"Great," Mr. Hollinger said. "Try to mix in some breaking balls with your fastballs, and you're sure to strike out the batters."

Adam practiced, throwing a perfect change-up. In fact, it was such a good pitch, his father missed it and the ball bounced off his glove and hit him gently on the head.

Corgi Capers: Deceit on Dorset Drive

"Great pitch," Mr. Hollinger said. "But it's getting a little dark, and I can't see. Let's head inside."

"Alright," Adam groaned.

Being outside and pitching had taken his mind off of all the stress from the burglary.

"Besides," Mr. Hollinger added. "I'm sure your puppy misses you. I bet Courtney's does too."

Adam rolled his eyes at the thought of his irresponsible sister.

Mr. Hollinger took off his glove.

"I know Courtney gives you a hard time," he told Adam. "You just have to take it with a grain of salt. She's becoming a teenager now, and it's something we'll all have to deal with."

Adam frowned.

"But Mom and I are proud of you. You're responsible and smart. That's why we let you have a dog. And I hope I can count on you to look after Courtney's dog, too. I mean, at least keep an eye out for trouble like what happened today in the junk room."

Adam nodded. Though it wasn't fair he had to look after his sister's puppy, he appreciated his father's confidence. Still, Adam frowned.

"What's the matter?" Mr. Hollinger asked.

"I have to tell you something. But I don't want you to get mad at me, or at the

Corgi Capers: Deceit on Dorset Drive

person who I tell you about."

"Okay," Mr. Hollinger said after a pause. "I promise."

Adam squinted. Grown-ups always said things like that, but there was no telling whether Mr. Hollinger would really get mad or not. Still, this was a secret Adam knew he shouldn't keep. He took a deep breath and then told Mr. Hollinger his discovery.

"I was looking on eBay to find a re-placement for the comic book the dogs tore apart. After that I ran a search for some of the things that were missing. A necklace like Mom's shell one came up from a seller who's shipping from Stoney Brook. And if you look at other items this person is selling, a lot of them are all things we own — or used to own."

Mr. Hollinger was frowning, and Adam wasn't sure he was doing the right thing. Was his father mad at him?

"There's more," Adam said. "When Courtney and I were walking the dogs, we bumped into the Davenports." Adam pointed to their house. "Their garage is like a huge warehouse where they have boxes and boxes of stuff. When we asked them about it, they said they have an online business. They sell their stuff online. I was just thinking...it seemed like too much of a coincidence. I think they may be the burglars."

"That's a very serious accusation," Mr. Hollinger said.

Corgi Capers: Deceit on Dorset Drive

"I know."

"If you accuse them, and you're wrong, it's going to be very uncomfortable living right down the street from them."

"I know, Dad. But I had to tell you."

Mr. Hollinger nodded. "You did the right thing, telling me. Why don't we go inside? You can show me this mysterious seller on eBay, and tomorrow maybe I can go and investigate the Davenport's garage myself."

Corgi Capers: Deceit on Dorset Drive

~ TWENTY-THREE ~
A Clue on the Computer

While Adam and his dad played catch, Courtney sat downstairs with the puppies. She put them each in their beds and sat at the computer typing instant messages to her friends.

While her back was turned from the puppies, Sapphie snuck out of her bed and approached her brother.

"Zeph, I don't like my bed. Can I stay in yours?"

Zeph growled softly. "Courtney told us to *stay*. Do you know what that means?"

"I don't care what it means. I'm a *princess!* I don't like the bed she put me in. I need room to stretch my legs and those dumb walls make it really hard."

"Well then curl up instead. I *love* curling up."

Sapphie protested. "Right now I feel like stretching. Can't I stay in your bed for a bit? I'm a princess. I get to do whatever I want."

Zeph signed. "Sapphie, there's something more important I need to talk to you about."

"What?"

"It's about that little incident today."

"Oh, you must mean the newspapers. Oh, Zeph, you should have smelled all the in-

Corgi Capers: Deceit on Dorset Drive

teresting scents in that room!"

"I did," her brother said harshly. "While I was looking for you."

"I regret nothing," Sapphie said and climbed into Zeph's bed.

"You pulled a stack of newspapers down on yourself."

"So?"

"You could have been hurt."

Sapphie's eyes flashed with just a moment of fear. Then she returned to her normal, capricious self. "But I wasn't hurt."

"That's not the point."

"You sound just like Pa."

"Good. *Someone* has to keep an eye on you." Zeph smiled to himself as he remembered the conversation Owl had with him. *Look out for her,* Owl's voice echoed in Zeph's mind.

Sapphie was already dozing off to sleep, but Zeph nudged her with his nose. She rolled over and covered her face with her paws, but her brother towered over her and used his own paws to nudge her.

"What already?" Sapphie asked. "Your bed is so comfortable. Leave me be! I just want to sleep."

"Not yet. First we need to talk about what happened."

"We already talked. You said I could have been hurt. I said I wasn't. End of story." Sapphie snuggled back in to the bed.

"Sapphie, it wasn't a good idea to go

Corgi Capers: Deceit on Dorset Drive

wandering around the house without your Person to make sure you're okay."

"Gee, it's not like I'm a baby or anything."

Zeph sighed. "You're not far from it." But he could see Sapphie was only half listening. She was distracted by a tiny gnat that was flying near her head. "Are you even listening?" Zeph asked.

"Yes, already. You said listen to people. Don't have any fun. Boy, Zeph. For such a young pup, you sure sound like an old dog!" And with that she pushed her brother out of the way, stretched out in the rocket ship bed, and closed her eyes.

Zeph walked over to the princess bed. He curled up in it, resting his head on the powder blue wall that encircled the bed. "Actually," he whispered to no one in particular, "this bed is comfortable. Very comfortable indeed."

~ * ~

Mr. Hollinger and Adam came in from the darkening twilight to find Courtney at the computer.

"There's a movie on that I want to see," Courtney announced. "It's starting now. Noelle just told me about it." She pointed to the computer screen.

"Does that mean you're finished with the computer?" Adam asked.

"Yeah. Not that you have any friends to talk to," she said cruelly.

Corgi Capers: Deceit on Dorset Drive

Mr. Hollinger gave Courtney a disapproving look.

"There's more to computers than instant messages," Adam said.

"Yeah, like what? Chat rooms for nerds?"

"No. I'm about to show Dad that all of our missing things are being listed for sale online. I think we'll be able to find the burglar."

Mrs. Hollinger was just coming down the stairs, and her ears pricked. She hurried to the computer. Adam logged on to show his parents the mysterious seller.

In the meantime, Courtney turned on the television and found the right channel. "At least they didn't take our TV. Or the family computer," she said.

Mr. Hollinger frowned. He wished the burglar hadn't taken his office computer, either.

Seated at the family computer, Adam turned to watch the movie's opening credits. It looked like a love story about a princess.

"It looks captivating," he said sarcastically.

"Shut up. You have to be sophisticated to enjoy a movie like this. It's not about robots or space aliens or anything like that." Courtney's phone buzzed. "I put it on vibrate so the text messages wouldn't interrupt me during the movie. This way I can just check them during commercials."

Corgi Capers: Deceit on Dorset Drive

Adam rolled his eyes. He doubted Courtney could wait until a commercial before sending a text message. Sure enough, her fingers were flying on the phone's keypads even while the opening scene was playing.

"Aileen's watching too!" Courtney announced, then turned up the volume.

Adam turned back to the computer screen and did a search for a seller with the screen name of SnowTown1877.

"There's some of the same video games that got stolen," Adam said.

"There *are*," Mrs. Hollinger corrected, tapping frantically on the screen.

"There's my coin collection, taken from my chest of drawers," Mr. Hollinger said.

"And there," Mrs. Hollinger said with a mix of horror and delight in her voice. "Is my seashell necklace!" She gasped. "He spelled necklace wrong — he wrote 'n-e-c-k-l-e-s-s.' How horrible!"

Mr. Hollinger didn't hesitate. He went right to the phone and called Officer Dunlap, the policeman who had been to the house earlier. He explained the situation, giving the name of the seller and some other details. A few minutes later, he returned.

"What did the police say?" Adam asked. "Can they catch the thief?"

"Can they get back my necklace?" Mrs. Hollinger asked.

"They'll try everything they can," Mr. Hollinger said. "They'll try to find the thief's

Corgi Capers: Deceit on Dorset Drive

identity. But don't get your hopes up. Sometimes these criminals are pretty sneaky, especially if they've stolen people's identities. At least that's what the police said."

"What about my necklace?" Mrs. Hollinger asked.

"The police said there's no guarantee it won't get sold to someone else. If you really want it back," Mr. Hollinger sighed, "you might want to bid on it."

"Place a bid on my own necklace?" Mrs. Hollinger mused. "I guess I don't have a choice."

"Still," Mr. Hollinger said sadly.

"Still what?" Mrs. Hollinger asked, already pushing Adam out of the way to use the computer. Even though she had to pay for her own necklace, she seemed happy to know that it was safe.

"Still," Mr. Hollinger continued. "The police said it will be difficult to prove that these items are actually ours. There's nothing that makes them unique. Those coins could be anybody's. The video games, too. And even the necklace. Truth be told, there are probably lots of similar necklaces in the world."

Mrs. Hollinger's eyebrows arched angrily. "I *know* my necklace."

Mr. Hollinger put a hand on her shoulder. "I know you do, Susan. But the police said we'll need a way to prove that those items are ours."

Adam sighed with frustration. He felt

Corgi Capers: Deceit on Dorset Drive

so close to catching the burglar. There had to
be a way to prove that those items were his.
He turned to find his detective hat and caught
sight of the puppies.

"Zeph!" Adam shrieked.

The family turned to look at Adam and
the puppies. The way Adam sounded, they
expected to see a ghost.

Instead, all they saw was Zeph in the
princess bed and Sapphie in the rocket ship
bed.

"What's wrong?" Mrs. Hollinger asked
from the computer.

"Don't you see?" Adam asked.

"See what?" said Mr. Hollinger.

"Can't you be quiet, Stupid?" Courtney
asked. "You're ruining the movie."

"Zeph is in the *princess* bed," Adam
explained. He said it like it was a horrible dis-
ease.

"So what?" Mr. Hollinger said. "If the
dogs like to switch beds, then let them be
happy."

"But Zeph's in a girl's bed."

But Mrs. Hollinger had already turned
back to the computer. Courtney was watching
the love story unfold on the screen, and Mr.
Hollinger was jotting something down on a little notepad.

"Well I won't stand for this. I'm taking
Zeph for a walk."

Adam got Zeph's harness — the one the
suspicious Davenports had given him — and

called Zeph, who happily trotted to the door
and allowed Adam to place the harness over
his head. He didn't even try to bite at it.

"Can you take Sapphie along?" Courtney asked.

"Come on, Sapphie," Adam called.

Sapphie took one look at the situation
and decided to stay put. If Courtney wasn't
going, then neither was she. She snuggled
deeper into the rocket ship bed and shut her
eyes.

"I tried," Adam said.

"Bring a flashlight," Mrs. Hollinger
called from the computer. "And don't go far.
It's dark out."

"And don't be too late," Mr. Hollinger
called. "We'll get up early tomorrow to practice some more pitching before your try-
outs."

"Right," Adam said. He'd almost forgotten that try-outs for pitching were tomorrow. All the excitement was a distraction, and
Adam hoped he'd be able to focus enough to
do well tomorrow. With that thought, he
grabbed the flashlight and headed out the
door.

~ TWENTY-FOUR ~
The Stranger in the Dark

The Hollingers lived in an old neighborhood. Not one house was younger than forty years old — and many were much older than that. The neighborhood had been built in an era before streetlights, and it was only through constant requests that the residents of Dorset Drive convinced the town to put in two lights: one at the cul-de-sac and one at the intersection that led out of the neighborhood. As a result, walking around at night was a very dark task.

At first Adam tested his bravery by walking without the flashlight. Here and there light from a front porch spilled onto the road. Still, as he looked up, the trees took on sinister shapes. When the wind blew, a giant oak looked like a three-armed monster reaching out to grab him. And there was just enough of a crescent moon to show the filmy clouds hovering spookily in the sky, veiling the stars in a gossamer shade.

Adam shivered and turned on his flashlight. He felt like it was Halloween.

Zeph, on the other hand, was not afraid. His nose took over so that the darkness didn't bother him.

"You're braver than I am," Adam admitted as he shined the flashlight at the oak — just to make sure it was still an oak.

Corgi Capers: Deceit on Dorset Drive

With that, Zeph let out a long, low *groowwwl*.

"What is it?" Adam gulped.

Zeph froze, his nose pointed toward the cul-de-sac. A moment later, Adam heard the shuffle-shuffle-shuffle of feet.

"Is somebody there?"

Adam pointed his flashlight in the direction of the noise. A jogger dressed in dark clothing shielded his eyes from the flashlight.

"Do you mind?" asked the jogger in an energetic — almost nervous — voice.

"Sorry," Adam said. "You scared me. Why are you jogging in the dark?"

"It's the best time," the man said hastily.

Adam shined the flashlight again on the man, but the man covered his face.

"It's dangerous to be out in such dark clothing. Especially with a burglar on the loose."

Adam pointed the flashlight once more at the stranger but the man had already started jogging away.

Zeph let out a tiny bark as the man disappeared into the darkness. Adam had only caught a glimpse of him. His hair was dark, and his body fit, but his face looked familiar. Adam tried to place it.

"He looks like Mister Frostburg," Adam whispered to Zeph. "Maybe old man Frostburg has a son."

Corgi Capers: Deceit on Dorset Drive

Adam hurried back home, where Mrs. Hollinger was glued to the computer. "I'm the highest bidder so far," she announced, tapping the screen to show Adam a picture of her seashell necklace. "And I even sent the seller a message about the misspelling in the description."

"That's great, Mom," Adam said as he took the harness off of Zeph.

Zeph crawled into the princess bed, and Adam shook his head.

"Susan," Mr. Hollinger said. "Don't forget that the auction doesn't end for another three days. You can't sit at the computer screen the whole time."

"If I need to, I will. Thief or no thief, this was the first gift you ever gave me, and I'd pay a small fortune to get it back."

"That's what I'm afraid of," Mr. Hollinger said and turned to Adam. "You look like you've seen a ghost. What happened?"

"I saw a man jogging."

"Did he bother you?" Mrs. Hollinger asked, suddenly disinterested in the computer screen.

"No. First I thought it was a neighbor, but he wouldn't tell me his name. I shined the flashlight at him, but he hid his face."

"Maybe you shouldn't shine lights in people's faces," Courtney said with her usual attitude.

"I just wanted to see who it was."

Corgi Capers: Deceit on Dorset Drive

"The poor man was probably just trying to get some exercise," Mr. Hollinger said. "Maybe he works late."

"He was wearing all dark colors," Adam explained.

"That's a little odd," Mr. Hollinger admitted. "Usually a late-night jogger would wear a reflective vest or something."

Mrs. Hollinger seemed concerned. "Did you recognize him? Is he a neighbor?"

"I didn't get to look for more than a few seconds, but his face looked sort of like Mister Frostburg's. His hair was dark, though, and he was in good shape. So it couldn't be old Mister Frostburg — he walks with a cane. Maybe he has a son?"

"Hmmm." Mr. Hollinger thought about it. "Not that I know of. I'll ask him next time I see him. Maybe he has family visiting."

"Honey," Mrs. Hollinger said to Adam. "Maybe your imagination's playing tricks on you. You've been excited about getting the dogs...and upset about the comic book being torn up...and the house being broken into. And I know you're nervous about pitching try-outs tomorrow. Maybe it's just your mind playing tricks on you. It *is* dark out there..."

Mr. Hollinger nodded. "Maybe Mom's right. Maybe you should head off to bed."

It was 9:30, which would be late if it were a school night but this was summer. Adam often stayed up much later reading comic books. But the look on his parents' faces con-

Corgi Capers: Deceit on Dorset Drive

vinced him otherwise. Besides, he needed his rest if he was going to make pitcher.

"Tomorrow," Mr. Hollinger said. "We can get up early and practice some pitching. Then I'll take a walk over to the Davenports' house and just check things out."

Adam nodded.

"And then pitching try-outs!" Mr. Hollinger added.

Adam tried to smile.

"Goodnight."

"Goodnight."

Adam put Zeph in his crate with a chew toy and a blanket before heading up to bed himself. Although Adam fell asleep quickly, Zeph sat awake, waiting for his sister to be put to bed. He had an idea that he just had to talk about.

~ TWENTY-FIVE ~
A Puppy Plan

"What a great movie," Sapphie told her brother. Courtney had just gone up to bed after putting Sapphie in her crate with a blanket and a cookie.

"I have an idea," Zeph said, ignoring his sister's banter.

"In the movie there was this girl who was really a princess but didn't know it. And she had to go around working like a normal person, and she just didn't seem to fit in. But then in the end she finds out she's a princess and she meets a prince, and they get married, and they live happily ev — "

"Do you even listen when I talk?" Zeph interrupted.

"Do *you* even listen when *I* talk? I was just telling you about the best movie Courtney and I watched. It's about this girl who was really a princess but..."

Zeph growled as Sapphie summarized the plot a second time. "Well, that certainly sounds like an interesting story," Zeph said, even though he didn't really think so.

"It was. Too bad you missed it."

"Anyway, Sapphie," Zeph said, trying to be as patient as possible. "Have you been following what's happening around the neighborhood?"

"Of course I have."

Corgi Capers: Deceit on Dorset Drive

"Good."

"But just in case, why don't you go over it again for me?"

Zeph sighed. "You understand that our People's house has been burglarized, right?"

"Yeeees. Stuff is missing. Duh!"

"Right," Zeph said, thankful she at least partially understood what was happening. "And they're not sure who the thief is."

"So?"

"So I think I know."

"Everyone knows. Didn't you hear them talking about it? Those people — the Davenports. They're the ones who stole all the stuff. They gave us those stupid harnesses to wear. Those harnesses make it so much more difficult to pull Courtney to where I want to go."

"Dogs aren't supposed to pull on walks."

"Bor-ing," Sapphie yawned.

"Fine," Zeph said. "But I know that the Davenports can't be the thieves."

"Why not?"

"They just don't seem like thieves. They seem friendly. And all the smells coming from their garage are friendly smells. Not mean smells. Besides, they were just trying to help our People."

"Fine, then. If you're so smart, who is the thief?"

Zeph smiled and sat up straight, puffing out his chest with pride. "The real thief is

Corgi Capers: Deceit on Dorset Drive

that bad man who came up to the porch. Frostburg, I think they called him."

"Frostburg? That old man? There's no way he could break into a house and then break out again with all that stuff."

"I wouldn't be too sure."

"What proof do you have?" Sapphie asked.

"Well, when we were downstairs I was sniffing around the family room, and I got to the part right near the broken window."

"So?"

"So that's where the burglar broke in."

"So?"

"So, I picked up a scent."

"What scent?"

"It was very faint. But I smelled it. It smelled just like Mr. Frostburg. I don't like that man's smell. When he was on the porch I just wanted him to leave."

"I don't like that stick he carries around," Sapphie said.

"His cane?"

"Yes, I hate that cane. I only got to bite a little piece, but if he comes around here again, I'll get the rest of it."

Zeph nodded. "Tonight, outside on the walk, Adam and I saw a man that looked just like him. Only younger. He smelled like he was up to no good."

"If he was younger, then how could it be the old man?"

Corgi Capers: Deceit on Dorset Drive

"It *smelled* like him. Maybe he's from the same house as Frostburg. Or maybe the old man *does* have a son." Zeph trailed off in thought.

"Zeph," Sapphie said finally.

"What?"

"You worry too much."

"No, I don't. I have reason to worry."

"Why is that?"

"Because I think that tomorrow morning, our People are going to accuse the wrong people."

"Well maybe you should go smell that mean man once more. Just to be sure."

"I can't, Sapphie. How would I get into his house?"

"Not my problem." Sapphie rolled on her back. Zeph sat in silence while Sapphie stared at the wall. "Although," she said finally. "I did get that piece of his cane."

"What piece?"

Sapphie rolled over and crunched on a cookie before answering. "The piece I pulled off his cane the day he came onto our porch. I buried it in the backyard. I'll give it to you tomorrow if you give me your cookie tonight."

"Why didn't you tell me about this earlier?" Zeph asked.

"How was I supposed to know you were crazy about catching this guy?"

Zeph huffed. "Here," he said, taking his cookie in his mouth and tossing it up. It went through the bars of his crate, into the air, and into Sapphie's crate. It landed on her head.

Sapphie barked contentedly before eating her second cookie and rolling over to sleep. She slept soundly the whole night.

Zeph, on the other hand, turned around in his crate to stare out the window at the moon. He had to help his People, and he needed to think of a plan, even if it meant staying up all night.

~ * ~

Much later that night, in the wee hours of the morning, Courtney awoke to an odd sound. She crept to her doorway to peek and could barely believe her eyes. Her father was carrying out bundles and bundles of old newspapers from his junk room. She heard him walk down two flights of stairs, all the way into the garage, where she heard the *thud* of the newspapers being tossed into the recycling bin. She fell back to sleep with a smile on her face.

When Mr. Hollinger stopped at the kitchen sink to wash off the newsprint from his hands, he saw that Zeph was still awake.

"Here boy, want a midnight snack?"

He handed Zeph a cookie. Zeph's tail wagged as he crunched his treat in the quiet moonlit kitchen.

~ TWENTY-SIX ~
Strike One

The next morning, Adam woke up early. He was nervous, and he had two good reasons. First, today was the day that Mr. Hollinger would walk to the Davenport's house. Second, today was the day of the pitching tryouts. In fact, that gave him a third reason to be nervous. Patrick would be at practice, and Adam would have to confess to the comic book getting chewed up. With that thought Adam rolled over and pulled the covers over his eyes. He wished he could stay in bed all day.

"You awake?" Mr. Hollinger asked, knocking on the door.

Adam groaned.

"I thought we could practice some pitching before it got to be too late. You don't want to tire yourself out too close to practice."

Adam groaned again.

"Come on, Sport!"

"Okay, okay."

Courtney was still sleeping, so Adam took the puppies outside in the fenced-in backyard.

Sapphie ran in fast, wild circles around Adam, barking each time she reached the pine tree. Zeph chased his sister for a while, but he soon grew tired of it and sat at Adam's feet, panting.

"I hope I did the right thing," Adam said. "I don't want to get the Davenports in trouble if they aren't the thieves. They'll be so mad at me..."

Zeph gave Adam's leg a little nudge, and Adam squatted down to pet the dog. As he did so, Sapphie ran up behind him and used Adam's back as a springboard to jump high into the air. She fell, tumbling to the ground with a yelp.

Before Adam could pick her up, she was running in circles again, barking as happily as ever. While Adam was watching Zeph, Sapphie snuck into the corner of the yard and dug up the piece of rubber cane tip she had buried.

"Sapphie, no!" Adam yelled, looking at the messy puppy. "No digging! Bad puppy!" Sapphie's paws were full of dirt, which the cool morning dew turned into mud.

Sapphie dropped the scrap of rubber near Zeph, then rolled over onto her back so Adam could pick her up. He carried her to the kitchen so she wouldn't track dirt into the house. Meanwhile, Zeph took the scrap of rubber and trotted into the house behind Adam.

"Good morning, Adam." Mrs. Hollinger greeted her son from the kitchen table where she was drinking coffee. At the sight of the muddy puppy, her eyes bulged open. "What happened to Sapphie?"

"Digging," Adam said.

Corgi Capers: Deceit on Dorset Drive

Mrs. Hollinger sighed. "Let's wash off her paws."

She went to the sink and removed her wedding ring as she always did before washing the dishes. Adam held the squirming puppy. Sapphie yapped and yapped. When Mrs. Hollinger turned on the water, she barked even louder.

"Quiet, Sapphie," Adam told the struggling puppy.

Mrs. Hollinger took the pull-out nozzle and squirted Sapphie's paws as Adam held her over the sink. Immediately, Sapphie stopped barking and struggling. She pawed at the water, sprinkling water and mud on Adam and Mrs. Hollinger. When she tired of that, she tried to drink the water from the faucet.

"I guess she likes water," Mrs. Hollinger said when they had finished cleaning her. "Now *I* need a shower!"

Zeph sat on the floor watching them. Every once in a while, he let out a quiet *howl*.

Mrs. Hollinger helped Adam towel-dry Sapphie. Although she liked water, she did *not* like towels. She bit at the towel and cried and groaned until Adam put her down. Mrs. Hollinger shook her head and hurried upstairs to rinse off in the shower.

Adam poured himself a glass of orange juice and sat down. He heard his dad downstairs and knew he'd soon want to help Adam warm up for the try-outs.

Corgi Capers: Deceit on Dorset Drive

"I wish I could figure out a way to prove that those things on eBay are ours," he muttered to himself.

On the floor, Zeph sat at Adam's side and nuzzled his leg.

"But those video games and the coins and even Mom's seashell necklace didn't have anything to identify them as ours. The police will never be able to catch the thief!"

Zeph ran to the sink and barked and barked. Adam got up and followed him.

"What, Zeph?" Adam asked.

Zeph stood on his hind legs, reaching toward the sink. He howled and howled and barked and barked.

"You want a bath, too?" Adam asked.

Zeph sat down and quieted.

"Guess not," Adam said. "Want some water?"

Zeph remained quiet.

Adam picked him up and showed him the sink. "What do you want, boy?"

Zeph sniffed and sniffed until he found Mrs. Hollinger's wedding ring. Then, he started barking.

"I don't understand," Adam said, putting Zeph on the floor. It was unlike Zeph to be so fussy. "What do you want with Mom's wedding ring?" Adam put down the barking pup and picked up the ring. "Why would you want a wedding ring?"

Then, a light bulb went off in his brain. "Of course. Mrs. Pinkney's ring! Thanks,

Corgi Capers: Deceit on Dorset Drive

Zeph," Adam yelled as he bounded down the steps to the computer downstairs.

~ * ~

Outside, Mr. Hollinger was waiting with the gloves. "Everything okay? I thought you got lost," he joked.

Adam threw a few warm-up pitches. "I had to check something on the computer. I found a way to identify the goods as ours."

"Oh yeah?"

"Remember the ring Mrs. Pinkney described?"

"Yes. White gold. Like the ocean. Something like that."

"And the inscription inside: *the ocean eternal, like our love.* I found it on eBay. It's listed by the same seller. SnowTown1877."

"Wow." Mr. Hollinger took off his glove to check his watch. "I guess it's still too early. I'll call Officer Dunlap once we're done."

He smiled as he tossed some warm-up throws to Adam. "I'm proud of you, Son," he said finally.

Adam smiled and pitched better than ever. The air was a perfect combination of the warm morning sun and the cool morning breeze. He heard the wind whooshing past his ear as he released the ball and the *snap* of the ball hitting his father's mitt.

After a while, Mr. Hollinger waved. "Bring 'er in." He patted Adam on the shoulder. "You're doing awesome, but we don't want to tire you out before try-outs. Besides, my hand is still stinging from catching some of those pitches!"

Adam smiled and led the way inside, where a delicious smell greeted them from the kitchen.

"Blueberry pancakes," Adam said.

Even Courtney seemed in a better mood.

"Adam was pitching like a pro," Mr. Hollinger announced.

"Was he?" Mrs. Hollinger smiled, though she still seemed glum.

"Yep. He'll do great at try-outs today. And these pancakes smell delicious."

Mrs. Hollinger's smile faded. Even Adam could tell something was wrong. "Honey," she said to her husband. "While you were playing catch with Adam, Todd Dunlap called."

"Did he?"

The table went silent.

"He tracked down the registered user behind username SnowTown1877."

"And?"

"A dead end."

"A dead end?"

"The person registered with false information. A fake name. A fake address. They traced the computer he — or she — used to the public library downtown. And those computers are open to everyone. So it could be anyone."

Corgi Capers: Deceit on Dorset Drive

"And the bank account he's been using?"

"Already been closed."

"That's a shame," Mr. Hollinger said. "Adam even found Mrs. Pinkney's ring listed for sale." Mr. Hollinger picked up the phone. "Maybe I should call her…so she can bid on her own ring."

"Well, nothing can help me with my seashell necklace. The officer said it's just too common. There's nothing unique about it. We can't prove that it's mine." Mrs. Hollinger sniffed away a tear.

Even Courtney frowned. Then her eyes sparkled with an idea.

"Hey, Mom," she said. "Do you think Adam will do *good* at his try-out today?" Her eyes flashed, waiting for her mother to correct her grammar.

"Do *well*," Mrs. Hollinger whispered automatically. But she still didn't smile.

Courtney looked at Adam with a shrug that said, "I tried."

Adam eyed his detective hat on the counter, wondering if there was a way he could help. Then he remembered.

"Here," he said, grabbing the hat. He retrieved the photograph from inside the hat's lining. "I found this picture in the basement."

Mrs. Hollinger held the photo and stared at the image of her seashell necklace.

Corgi Capers: Deceit on Dorset Drive

"Maybe there's something in the picture that can help," Adam suggested.

But the picture only seemed to make his mother more upset. She handed it back to him.

"Wait," Adam said, studying the picture carefully. He grabbed a magnifying glass from the kitchen desk. "Look at this." He pointed. "See this little notch?"

In the corner of the seashell, there was a tiny piece missing. It looked like the shell had been chipped.

"I'd forgotten about that," Mrs. Hollinger said. She grabbed the picture and ran downstairs to the computer. Adam followed, and so did Courtney and their father.

Mrs. Hollinger's fingers flew across the keyboard as she navigated to the page selling the seashell necklace.

"Aha!" she said. "There it is. The picture online is identical to the one in this photograph. The same chip is missing from both seashells. This picture is proof enough. I knew it — I knew this was my seashell necklace!"

She turned to Adam. "Thanks for finding the picture. I had forgotten all about it."

Adam winked at Courtney before turning back to his mother. "I did *good*, huh?"

Mrs. Hollinger smiled, catching onto the joke. "You did *well*," she corrected with a grin.

Corgi Capers: Deceit on Dorset Drive

The family returned to their breakfast upstairs. In between bites of pancakes, Mr. Hollinger paused.

"When you talked to the police, did Officer Dunlap mention anything about the Davenports? Last night I told him about their garage full of goods for sale," he said.

Mrs. Hollinger looked up from her breakfast and the picture of the necklace that she had displayed right next to her plate.

"He did mention that. He's trying to get a warrant, but he's not sure there's enough evidence. He said he'd be here around three o'clock, and he'll walk over with you. If he can't get a warrant, all we can do is request that the Davenports show us what they have for sale."

"And the Davenports can always refuse," Mr. Hollinger concluded.

Mrs. Hollinger nodded. "But just think: my seashell necklace could be just down the street. So close, but so far..."

Adam's heart sank. With all this talk of warrants and police, he felt guilty for getting the Davenports involved. The more he thought about it, the less sure he was that they were the culprits. He'd even lost his appetite for pancakes. It was already nearly ten o'clock — only two hours until the tryouts — and the last thing in the world Adam felt like doing was pitching.

~ TWENTY-SEVEN ~
A Change of Heart

The boys were excited for practice. Nearly half the team wanted to try out for pitcher. During warm-ups, the boys lined up by number, so Adam and Patrick stood next to each other: Adam was number seven, and Patrick was number eight. For once, Adam wished he were not standing so close to his best friend. He hoped Patrick didn't mention the comic book so he could avoid the topic until *next* practice.

"Did you get to finish the comic book?" Patrick asked as they waited their turn to run the bases.

Adam's heart sank. "No."

"You've had it for two whole days!"

"I know, but a lot has happened. Our house was burglarized."

"That's terrible! You should have called me."

"I would have, but..."

"But what?"

In truth, Adam had been avoiding Patrick since the comic book mishap. But Adam didn't want to tell Patrick that. Not yet.

"We also got two puppies. I've been busy."

"Two puppies! You *really* should have called me. I want to see them."

Corgi Capers: Deceit on Dorset Drive

Adam frowned. He hated being dishonest. He also didn't want to get Patrick mad before the try-outs since Patrick was trying out for pitcher, too.

"Patrick."

"Yes?"

"There's something I need to tell you about that comic book."

"Number seven!" Coach Harris called.

Adam breathed a sigh of relief. "That's me," he said and hurried down the baseline, never happier to run warm-ups.

After warm-ups, the boys hurried to their positions. Coach Harris rotated pitchers and hitters to allow all the boys a chance to try out as pitcher. Adam was the second boy to bat. He didn't get to swing at all: the first four pitches were all balls. Ryan wasn't very good at pitching. In fact, practice was boring, with just a few pitchers good enough to throw consistently over home plate.

When it was Adam's turn to pitch, he was more nervous than he'd ever been. Besides worrying about pitching, he couldn't stop thinking about the Davenports and Mr. Frostburg and the image of Patrick's comic book torn to shreds all over the kitchen floor.

"Ball one!" Coach Harris called after Adam's first pitch. "A little low, Hollinger."

Adam tried to shake off his nerves and pretend he was just outside his front yard pitching to his dad.

Corgi Capers: Deceit on Dorset Drive

"Stree—ike!" Coach Harris called. "Nice curveball, Hollinger."

Adam smiled and continued to picture himself in his neighborhood. He thought about his dad's smile, the way the ball sounded as it whooshed out of his hand and down the street to his father's glove. He mixed fastballs and sliders to strike out the next two batters.

Coach Harris nodded in approval, and Adam's teammates cheered. Even Mr. Hollinger, who had stayed to watch Adam pitch, cheered from the bleachers.

Adam continued pushing out distractions — even all the cheers — from his mind. He imagined the way the trees in his neighborhood looked. He threw three curveballs. He imagined the peaceful way the sun set behind the hill across the street. He struck out the next batter.

Then he imagined Mr. Frostburg creeping his way down the hill, his cane raised threateningly at Adam. *"Don't you throw your balls at my yard!"* the old man scolded in Adam's memory.

Adam lost focus. His pitch was slow, and the batter scored a homerun.

"Nice work before you lost focus, Hollinger," Coach called when Adam's turn was done.

Adam smiled half-heartedly. He knew he'd done well, but he hadn't done his best. He was preoccupied with other things. He hoped his coach didn't think badly of him.

Corgi Capers: Deceit on Dorset Drive

After practice, Adam waited in line to see Coach Harris, who was talking to some of the parents. He wanted to explain why he'd been so distracted. After that, he told himself, he'd have to tell Patrick the truth. As he waited in line, Mr. Hollinger approached from the bleachers.

"Nice job, Adam," he said.

"Thanks, Dad, but I could have done better."

"You struck out two batters. That's not bad, in my book."

Before Adam could respond, Mr. Hollinger's cell phone rang.

"It's for you," he said after answering.

"For me? Who is it?"

"It's your sister."

Adam thought he must be dreaming. His sister would never, ever willingly call him.

"Hello?" Adam said cautiously.

"Adam?"

"Yeah?"

"Did you tell Patrick about the comic book yet?"

"No."

"Good. Don't."

"Why?"

"Listen. Last night, I was awake pretty late. And do you know what I saw?"

"No. What?"

"Make sure Dad doesn't hear, okay?" Courtney asked.

Corgi Capers: Deceit on Dorset Drive

Adam took a few steps away from his father. "Okay. What did you see?"

Adam's mind raced with possibilities. Did Courtney have new information about the burglar?

"Get ready, 'cause you'd never expect this in a million years!"

Adam's heart raced.

"Dad actually got rid of the newspapers in his junk room. I saw him!"

"Really?"

He sighed in disappointment because Courtney didn't have any information about the burglar. But she was right: Adam would never have guessed his father would clean out the junk room.

"But don't tell Dad I saw. Anyway, I was awake, and it was dark and quiet in the house, and I just kept thinking if Dad could do something good like that, maybe I could too."

"What are you talking about?"

Adam was used to Courtney's attitude and insults — not her thoughtfulness.

"Listen, I'm trying to do something nice, so just go with it. When the dogs chewed up your comic book, it was my fault. I tried to toss it on the kitchen table but missed. I saw it fall onto the floor. I saw it sitting there, right in reach of the puppies. I saw, but I just didn't care enough to go in and pick it up. See what I'm saying? It's my fault."

Corgi Capers: Deceit on Dorset Drive

"Thanks for admitting that," Adam said, still confused. "Does this mean *you're* going to tell Patrick?"

Courtney laughed. "Of course not! Something even better. I talked to Aileen, and she texted her dad, who's in the city today on business. Well, he stopped into a bookstore and got a copy of that stupid comic — limited edition, just like the one that got ruined — for thirty dollars. He'll bring it tonight. All you gotta do is pay him back."

"Thanks, Courtney."

"It's the least I can do." She cleared her throat and added. "I guess if I ever get another babysitting job, I can try to pitch in. You know, for the cost."

Adam smiled. By the time he hung up the phone, Coach Harris was already in his car. Adam decided he didn't need to talk to him after all.

But apparently Coach had something to say to Adam. From his car he called, "Hollinger. Nice job today. I'll make my decision soon!"

"Thanks!" Adam waved to his coach.

"Adam?" Patrick called from the car. "What was it you wanted to tell me about the comic book?"

Adam smiled. "I'll have it back to you soon."

One day, he promised himself, he'd tell Patrick the truth. But for now, it could wait.

Corgi Capers: Deceit on Dorset Drive

~ TWENTY-EIGHT ~
Strike Two

When Adam and Mr. Hollinger arrived at the house, Officer Dunlap was already on the front porch speaking to Mrs. Hollinger.

She tried to smile when Adam arrived, but her eyes looked sad.

"Honey," she said. "Courtney went to Aileen's house, and she left the puppies in the kitchen. Unsupervised. Would you mind watching them?"

Adam nodded, but something was strange. The Hollingers had left the puppies alone in the kitchen before, at least for a few minutes. So why was his mother concerned now? Everyone remained quiet until Adam had gone inside. Then, he heard muffled voices on the porch. Finally he understood: his mother didn't want him to hear whatever was being said.

He went up to the kitchen. The two puppies were busy playing tug-of-war with a plush mailman toy. As soon as Zeph saw him, he dropped the toy and ran over, his stubby tail raised as high as it would go. Sapphie, on the other hand, used the distraction as an opportunity to gain full possession of the plush toy. She happily squeaked it and ran around the kitchen in three big circles before running up to greet Adam.

"Listen, puppies. I know I just got here,

Corgi Capers: Deceit on Dorset Drive

but I need to sneak outside and figure out what's happening. Whatever it is, Mom doesn't want me to hear. I need you guys to go into your crates and be as quiet as possible." He tapped the cushions inside the crates. "Go ahead — into your Little Houses."

Zeph barked once, then jumped into his crate. He rather liked the security of it, the warm blankets, the chew toys — not to mention the peace and quiet from his sister. Sapphie took one look at her brother and let out a high-pitched bark.

"In your House," Adam told her firmly.

Sapphie barked again, then ran around the kitchen. Adam tried to grab her, but it was obvious that she had lured him into a game of chase — a game she was enjoying very much. Finally, she ran under the open dishwasher door panting hard.

Adam grabbed her gently, picked her up, and placed her in her crate. As he turned to leave, he put a finger to his lips and said, "Shhhh."

Sapphie responded with one single, shrill bark before plopping down to rest.

Adam crept into the entryway of the house. He pressed his head against the door so that he could hear Officer Dunlap.

"We couldn't get any information about this eBay seller," the officer was saying. "Other than the fact that he provided fraudulent information. Looks like he's stolen his fair share of wallets. All the information he

Corgi Capers: Deceit on Dorset Drive

used to register online came from people who reported their wallets stolen within the past month or so."

"So what can we do?" Mrs. Hollinger asked.

"Well, if you really think these neighbors of yours — the Davenports — may be the thieves, we can go over and request that they let us look around, but we couldn't get a warrant. We just don't have enough evidence." The policeman paused. "If they refuse, then we have to leave."

Adam felt terrible. The more he thought about it, the more he thought the Davenports were just a nice couple who happened to sell goods online. The fact that the police couldn't find enough evidence to secure a warrant only confirmed his suspicion. He couldn't keep it to himself any longer.

"Mom," he said, bursting out of the front door. "Dad."

His parents looked at him, bewildered. "Adam," Mrs. Hollinger said. "I thought you were inside watching the puppies."

Adam shook his head. "The puppies can watch themselves for a minute. I have to talk to you. I don't think the Davenports are the thieves. It's all just a big coincidence. Did you tell the police about the man I saw last night while I was walking Zeph?"

"What's this about a man?" Officer Dunlap asked.

"I saw this man jogging late at night.

Corgi Capers: Deceit on Dorset Drive

He wore dark clothing. He looked like an old man who lives over there." Adam pointed to Mr. Frostburg's house. "Only he was younger. Like maybe he was Mister Frostburg's son or something. Anyway, he seemed suspicious jogging in the dark like that, and he wouldn't let me see his face."

"Hmmm," Officer Dunlap considered, jotting down some notes on his notepad. "And how long has this Frostburg fellow been living in the neighborhood?"

"About three, four years now," Mr. Hollinger said. "But he's an old man. He can't walk without his cane. Adam has a very active imagination. Always reading his comic books."

"I'm telling you," Adam said. "There's something fishy about Mister Frostburg. Or his son."

"Oh, Adam," Mrs. Hollinger said and turned to the officer. "He's been stressed out lately. We just got two puppies, and he's had baseball try-outs, and of course the burglary."

"Baseball this late in the year?" Officer Dunlap asked.

"Autumn League," Adam said.

"Impressive!" Officer Dunlap nodded. "My nephew tried out for Autumn League. Didn't make it though. Maybe next year. When we're finished at the Davenports, we'll check out this mysterious jogger, son."

Adam smiled.

They must have looked quite intimidat-

ing walking down the Davenports' driveway—
Officer Dunlap, Mr. and Mrs. Hollinger, and
Adam tagging along even though everyone
asked him not to.

"Can we help you?" Mrs. Davenport
asked even before they rang the doorbell. "I
saw you walking down the drive," she explained. "It's not every day we get so many
visitors all at once."

The policeman shuffled his feet for a
moment before speaking. "We're investigating a series of burglaries."

"Oh, the serial burglar. I hope you
catch him. Or her," Mrs. Davenport added.
"We have lots of goods in our garage, and we
feel like we can't leave the house anymore.
We're afraid when we get back all our stuff
will be gone."

"What stuff is that, exactly?" Officer
Dunlap asked.

"Oh, we buy items from places like
secondhand shops and yard sales, and we sell
them online. We make a good profit, too. One
man's trash is another's treasure, they say."
She smiled warmly. "Can I offer anyone a
drink? Would you like to come inside?"

"Actually, ma'am," Officer Dunlap continued. "We were wondering if we could ask
you a few questions about your online business."

"Certainly. Let me get Frank. He does
more of the business side of things. I'm in
charge of posting everything for sale online. I

always did want to be a photographer."

She disappeared into the house and returned with her husband. "Let's all go out to
our warehouse," she said.

They followed her into the packed garage.

"We got a great closeout deal on lawn
chairs, and we're saving them to sell in the
spring, when demand goes up." She dug behind some boxes until she emerged with some
comfortable-looking chairs. "I think we have
enough for everyone."

Everyone took a seat. Adam's insides
felt terrible, just like the time years ago when
he accepted Courtney's dare to eat a peanut-
butter-and-worm sandwich.

"Now what kinds of things do you want
to know?" Mrs. Davenport asked.

"Well, there's been some speculation
that the serial burglar might be using online
venues to get rid of his stolen goods."

"How intriguing," Mrs. Davenport said.

"Quite," agreed her husband.

"Anyway," the officer continued.
"We'd like to ask you about your online business. We need a list of all the usernames you
use to sell your goods."

Mrs. Davenport smiled. "Just one.
Frankelle531."

"Frankelle531?" Officer Dunlap confirmed, recording the name.

"Frank plus Ellen. And we were married
on May 31. I won't tell you what year," she

joked. "It'll make me feel old!" She smiled at Adam.

"And these goods, you came by them all...legally?"

"Oh my!" Mrs. Davenport said. "Are we suspects?" She seemed more intrigued than angry, but Adam still felt guilty.

"Not exactly," the officer said. "But it is somewhat of a coincidence that the stolen goods are turning up online."

Mr. and Mrs. Davenport considered. "I guess I'd suspect us too," she said finally.

"Well, we have nothing to hide. You're free to look around. This is our warehouse." She motioned to the entire garage. "How exciting," she added, clapping her hands. "A real police investigation!"

They were such a nice couple that Mr. and Mrs. Hollinger hated what they were about to do. But they had to be sure. Adam shuffled toward home as Mr. Hollinger opened the first box.

Corgi Capers: Deceit on Dorset Drive

~ TWENTY-NINE ~
The Great Escape

In the kitchen, Zeph was quite agitated, even in the comfort and safety of his crate. He kept twirling and howling — like Owl.

"What's wrong with *you?*" Sapphie asked. "You're acting like *me.*"

"Adam needs our help. The wrong people are being accused, and no one believes Adam about that mean man we saw last night. I'm trying to find a way to help him, but I can't think of anything."

"How can *you* help?" Sapphie asked.

"I need to prove that the bad man — the one I saw last night — is the one behind the burglaries."

"What proof do you have?" Sapphie asked.

"That's the problem. I don't have any proof. Just my sense of smell. No one would believe that."

He found the scrap of rubber from the cane tip — he'd buried it under the blanket in his crate. He sniffed at it.

"What are you doing?" Sapphie asked.

"This scrap you took from that man on the porch smells *exactly* like the man Adam and I met while we were out for a walk last night."

Corgi Capers: Deceit on Dorset Drive

"So stop whining and get some evidence," Sapphie said, stretching. "If you're as smart as I think you are, finding evidence should be easy for you."

Zeph whined and plopped his head down on his front paws. "I'm out of ideas," he said.

Sapphie barked. "Are you really going to leave it to *me* to come up with a plan?"

"Do you have one?"

"I'm sure we'll find something at Frostburg's house."

"Are you forgetting?" Zeph asked.

"Forgetting what?"

"That we're stuck in these crates, not to mention stuck in this kitchen. And even if we could get out of here, we'd never get outside on our own. Besides, we're not allowed to leave without our People."

"Silly Zeph. Don't you know *anything*?"

With that, Sapphie sat on her hind legs and elevated her body so she looked like a kangaroo. Then she positioned her paw so it rested on the latch of her crate. With practiced dexterity, she pushed on the latch, slid it out of place with her teeth, and exited her crate.

"I've been practicing," she told Zeph as she reached for his latch and helped him escape.

"Okay," said Zeph. "You impressed me. But we're still stuck in the kitchen."

"Silly boy. You still don't trust my abilities." She brushed against his neck the way a cat would. "Follow me," she said.

Zeph followed.

Sapphie stopped at the safety gate. "Stay," she instructed.

Zeph did as he was told and trembled as Sapphie backed up to the other end of the kitchen, then took a running start right toward him.

"Stay, stay, *stay!*" she yelled.

Zeph stayed.

Things seemed to move in slow motion as Sapphie charged him, then jumped onto his back and used him as a springboard to clear the safety gate. She landed gingerly on the other side.

"Good job. But what about me?"

"Do you even have to ask anymore?" She pressed down on a lever of the gate with her two front paws. "It opens from *this* side."

The tension on the gate easily loosened, and the gate clattered to the floor. By the time Zeph realized he was free, Sapphie was already at the front door.

"Just as I suspected," she told Zeph, who was panting from running down the steps. "It's been left open. We only have to open the screen door."

"And you know how to do that?"

"I've been watching my Person. I'm going to need your help again."

Like before, Zeph stood stone-still at the door, and Sapphie took a running leap, using Zeph as a springboard to dive right for the door handle. She pushed it easily, and the door flew open.

"Quick!" Sapphie yelled, and Zeph made it out just before the screen door slammed shut again.

"I got us out," Sapphie said. "Now it's your turn."

"There's only one place we need to be," Zeph said, and he ran as fast as his little legs would carry him to old man Frostburg's house at the top of the hill.

Corgi Capers: Deceit on Dorset Drive

~ THIRTY ~
Double Trouble

Mr. and Mrs. Hollinger had been searching the Davenport's garage for a while now, and they hadn't found any stolen goods. Adam, feeling guilty, had shuffled down the street toward his house. But he'd changed his mind and returned to the Davenport's garage.

"They're not the burglars," Adam said. "They were kind enough to give us harnesses for the dogs..."

"Son, why don't you go home and play with your puppies?" Officer Dunlap suggested. "We'll make the conclusions once we finish searching."

"It's okay, Adam," Mr. Davenport said. "We understand. We're not mad."

"It's flattering, actually," said Mrs. Davenport. "We're suspects! What an exciting story we'll have to tell our family at Thanksgiving!"

Adam shook his head, stooped his shoulders, and shuffled toward home.

When he got there, he was shocked: the kitchen was empty. And so were the crates!

"Zeph!" Adam called. "Sapphie!"

But no bark answered his call. He checked the entire house, from the basement all the way to the junk room (which didn't look so junky anymore). No sign of the dogs.

Corgi Capers: Deceit on Dorset Drive

He was just leaving to check the yard when he heard a commotion from the hill across the street.

"Help!" a shaky old voice called.

It was Mrs. Stoy, and she was hobbling down her driveway toward the Hollinger's house.

"Where are the police?" she asked Adam.

Adam stood, bewildered.

"The police, Boy. The police!" she repeated. "There's a police car in your driveway. Where are the officers?"

Adam regained his ability to speak. "At the Davenports' house."

Mr. Stoy, with his walker, shuffled down the driveway after his wife.

For a moment, Adam forgot about the missing puppies and hurried after the Stoys, eager to see what the commotion was about.

"We've been robbed!" Mrs. Stoy shouted down the street. "The serial burglar has struck again!"

Officer Dunlap hurried out of the Davenport's garage and ran toward the Stoys.

"When?"

"Just now!" Mrs. Stoy shouted. "While we were out to lunch with our grandkids. We just got home, and we weren't gone but an hour."

"Right in the middle of the day," Mr. Stoy huffed.

Corgi Capers: Deceit on Dorset Drive

"Well, if the burglary just happened," Officer Dunlap said. "It isn't likely it's the Davenports. We've been here for nearly an hour already."

"I just don't understand it," Mrs. Stoy said sadly. "We locked all our doors. And that kindly Mister Frostburg even looked inside our house the other day to make sure our windows and doors were secure. He told us he couldn't think of anything else we could do to make our home any safer."

"Mister Frostburg, you say?" the officer asked, glancing at his notepad.

Mr. and Mrs. Hollinger looked at Adam. "Son?" asked Officer Dunlap. "Is that the same Mister Frostburg you were telling me about?"

"Maybe," Adam said. "But he looked younger last night."

Suddenly, Adam had a horrible feeling. He knew where the puppies were, and he knew they were in trouble!

~ THIRTY-ONE ~
Home Run

Mr. Frostburg's yard was lonely all the way on top of the hill. It was shady, too. It gave Sapphie the chills.

"I don't like it here," she told her brother.

The puppies crept along the side of Mr. Frostburg's house. They heard a door open in the back, and they jumped into the leafy Hostas for cover.

"That was close," Zeph whispered.

"The coast is clear," Sapphie said, jumping out of the leaves.

The two dogs sniffed and sniffed. They tried their hardest not to bark even though they recognized the mean smell that came from Mr. Frostburg. It smelled the same way a cawing crow sounds: creepy and unsettling.

But soon Zeph picked up a different scent. This scent smelled very faint, but...it smelled like his People! Zeph's tail wagged as he followed the scent to a large shed in the back yard. He forgot himself and let out three loud, resonant barks.

"Shhh," Sapphie said. "I can't believe *I'm* telling *you* to be quiet!"

"Sorry. It's just...I smell our People."

The shed door hung ajar, and Zeph snuck right in. It was packed with boxes. Some of them smelled like the Hollingers.

Corgi Capers: Deceit on Dorset Drive

Even Sapphie couldn't keep from barking this time. The puppies ran in circles around each other, celebrating.

"We found our People's missing stuff," Zeph said. "Maybe Dad's computer is here."

But before the puppies could find out, a shadow loomed over them. It was Mr. Frostburg — or a younger version of him, anyway.

He was dressed in dark clothing, and his hair was dark, his body svelte, and he walked without a cane.

"You rodents," he cried. "Get out of here."

He was carrying a box of items, which he placed on the floor. Then, he took a silver lamp and swung at the dogs. He hit Zeph's hindquarter, and the puppy winced in pain, yelping from the blow.

"Zeph!" a boy's voice called from the street.

"Stupid rodents. I said get out!"

But the dogs would not budge. They ran behind a box that smelled like their People, and they refused to come out.

"Zeph! Sapphie!" The boy's voice was getting closer.

Mr. Frostburg stormed out of the shed, closing and latching the door. The two trembling puppies were locked inside.

"Mister Frostburg," Adam said, running toward the shed and trying to sound normal. "Have you seen my puppies?"

Corgi Capers: Deceit on Dorset Drive

"No." The man hurried toward his house. He pulled up his collar, pulled down his baseball cap, and kept his head low.

"Mister Frostburg," Adam said. "Where's your cane? And what happened to your hair?"

"Bah!" he groaned and continued inside. "Get off my property or I'm calling the cops."

When Mr. Frostburg spoke in such a harsh tone, Adam didn't feel like being polite anymore.

"Go ahead. Call them. There's an officer right down the street."

Mr. Frostburg took one look down the hill and saw Officer Dunlap, Mr. and Mrs. Hollinger, Mr. and Mrs. Stoy, and Mr. and Mrs. Davenport walking up his driveway. He hurried into his house.

"Adam!" Mrs. Hollinger called. "Is everything all right? We heard you scream! And we heard puppies barking. Is everyone okay?"

From inside the shed, Adam heard a muffled bark.

"Zeph!" he called.

"Adam?" Mrs. Hollinger called again.

"Mom, I'm up here," Adam yelled. "I think the puppies are trapped somewhere."

Mr. Frostburg came outside again. His hair was gray now, he walked with a cane, and he sure didn't look friendly.

"Help!" Adam cried. "Mom! Dad! Help!"

Corgi Capers: Deceit on Dorset Drive

"Get off my property," Mr. Frostburg called again. He made his voice sound older. "You're trespassing."

Officer Dunlap charged up the driveway.

"You're not allowed on my property without a warrant," Mr. Frostburg yelled. "Get off."

"Mister Frostburg," the officer said. "There's a boy screaming, and I hear barking dogs from inside your shed. I'm within my rights."

Mr. Frostburg remained silent.

Crying and clawing echoed from inside the shed.

"Sir, we need you to open the shed."

"Get a warrant!" Frostburg shouted.

"I'll radio for an emergency warrant. But I'm staying right here to keep an eye on you. You know," he said to Mr. Frostburg. "Cooperation often looks better during a trial. You sure you don't want to let those dogs out of your shed?"

The anger in Mr. Frostburg's eyes turned slowly to defeat.

"It's my dog!" Adam screamed.

He rushed past the adults and threw open the shed door. Not even Mr. Frostburg tried to stop him. A moment later, Sapphie scrambled out with Zeph hobbling behind her. He limped and whined, his back leg held up in pain.

Corgi Capers: Deceit on Dorset Drive

"Stupid rodents," Frostburg muttered under his breath.

"Zeph!" Adam cried.

Zeph limped toward Mr. Frostburg, barking as loudly as he could.

Sapphie followed Zeph's lead and stalked Mr. Frostburg, backing him onto his patio. Sapphie let out a final growl, and Mr. Frostburg backed right into a lawn chair. He toppled over, muttering as he fell. When he stood, a gray wig fell halfway off his head.

"Jim?" Mr. Hollinger asked. "Jim, I thought you were an old man! You always walked around with a cane and a hat and..."

"These types are tricky," Officer Dunlap told Mr. Hollinger. "They can live in your neighborhood for years, gaining your trust, doing their research. Then, when you least expect it, they strike."

"You have to understand," young Mr. Frostburg cried. "I made some bad investments and lost everything. I needed a way to make my money back. Besides, what harm did it do? You all have homeowner's insurance. They would have paid for the missing items."

"But that wouldn't replace my seashell necklace," Mrs. Hollinger said.

"Or my clients' information," Mr. Hollinger said.

"Or Eden Pinkney's grandmother's ring," Mrs. Hollinger added.

"Let's go." Officer Dunlap slapped handcuffs on Mr. Frostburg. "Adam," he said.

"Yes, Sir?" Adam looked up from Zeph's wounded leg.

"Good job on the case."

"Thanks."

"Oh, and kid?"

"Yes, Sir?"

"Good luck with that Autumn League!"

~ THIRTY-TWO ~
Girls!

The Hollingers were busy during their last week of summer vacation. They had to go to the police station to claim their valuables, and they still had cleaning up to do. Adam had baseball practice, and Zeph had to see the vet about his injured hind leg. Worst of all, they had to go back-to-school shopping. Courtney loved buying new clothes, but she hated all the school supplies. Adam was just the opposite. Yet both siblings were happy with the new backpacks Mr. and Mrs. Hollinger allowed them to pick out.

Two nights before school started, Courtney planned an end-of-summer sleepover with Aileen and Noelle. She was going to take over the family room with blankets, pillows, sleeping bags, and junk food...Which meant it was going to be a long night for Adam.

Adam watched from his bedroom window as Mrs. Ellison pulled into the driveway. He shuddered as he watched Mrs. Ellison, Aileen, *and* Marnie get out of the car and walk to the front porch. Aileen rang the doorbell, but her mother and Marnie remained there on the front porch, too.

"Why Marnie, of all people?" Adam asked Zeph, who rested on the bed with Adam.

Corgi Capers: Deceit on Dorset Drive

Zeph barked quietly.

"Adam!" Courtney shouted. "Can you get the door?"

Courtney was in the kitchen with Sapphie and Noelle. Adam wondered what she was doing that was so important she couldn't be bothered to answer the door.

Nonetheless, Adam did as she asked — as he usually did. Zeph stayed on Adam's bed, resting his injured hindquarter, so Adam was left to face the girls alone. He took a very deep breath and opened the door.

"Hi, Adam." Mrs. Ellison smiled. "I understand congratulations are in order. I heard your coach made you the alternate pitcher for your Autumn League team."

"Yeah," Adam said.

"Well I think that's great. It's tough to make Autumn League, let alone pitcher. Do you enjoy your new position?"

Adam's ears turned red. "Thanks, Missus Ellison. I do like pitching. And even as alternate pitcher, I get to pitch at least a few innings each game."

"Which homeroom teacher do you have next year?" Mrs. Ellison asked.

Adam had just gotten his schedule in the mail. "Miss Paulus. Room 112."

"Did you hear that, Marnie? Adam has Miss Paulus, too. Maybe you two can sit together."

Marnie rolled her eyes, then looked at Adam. "I heard Miss Wilkerson moved up a year. She's teaching fifth grade science, now, not fourth. Looks like we'll have her again this year. Bet you're happy to hear that!"

She made a kissing motion with her lips and giggled all the way to her mother's car, where she sat down and quickly started texting on her very own cell phone.

Adam sighed. He was hoping, of all things, to avoid starting the year off as the nerd, the teacher's pet. He was hoping that being a pitcher for the Autumn League might help his social status. And he was hoping Marnie Ellison wouldn't be in his class. He'd had enough of her pranks last year. But it looked like he was off to a rocky start — and school hadn't even started yet.

Aileen's phone buzzed. She read the text, looked at her mother's car, and made eye contact with her sister. Both girls giggled.

"I'm going to go find Courtney," Aileen said without saying goodbye to her mother.

Mrs. Ellison smiled as her daughter ran up the stairs. "Take it easy, Adam," she said. "Make sure those girls go easy on you. They can be a handful at this age."

"You can say that again." Adam sighed.

When Adam went inside, the three girls — Courtney, Aileen, and Noelle — had taken their places in the family room. Courtney hogged the love seat, Aileen stretched out on the couch, and Noelle leaned back in the recliner.

"Good grief," Adam muttered as he

Corgi Capers: Deceit on Dorset Drive

tried to slip up the stairs without being noticed.

"Adam!" Aileen called.

He poked his head down the stairwell.

"You probably think you're king of the
school now that you're a fifth grader, don't
you?"

Adam shrugged.

"Well don't let it go to your head.
'Cause fifth graders ain't nothin' but babies."

"And just wait for a year from now,"
Noelle added. "We'll all be in middle school
together."

"Yes," Aileen continued. "In one year
from now, we'll be eighth graders — queens of
the school. And you'll be a low-life sixth
grader, the baby of the school all over again."

The three girls laughed, and Adam
trudged up the stairs.

Later, Mrs. Hollinger made Adam eat
dinner with them. She'd ordered pizza and
told Adam that *"it would be a kind gesture"* if
he ate a few slices with the girls.

Adam shuddered to himself. Even the
delicious slices of pepperoni didn't seem
worth the risk of eating with the three girls.

"So Adam?" Aileen asked as they were
eating pizza. "Do you think my sister is cute?"

"Marnie?" Adam asked. "Cute?"

"Yeah. Like on a scale of one to ten,
where one is, like, totally ugly, and ten is,
like, more beautiful than a fashion model,

Corgi Capers: Deceit on Dorset Drive

where would you rank my sister?"

"I don't know," Adam said. Why did girls have to ask such dumb questions?

"That means you think she's really ugly. You just don't want to admit it because you'll hurt her feelings," Noelle teased.

"No, I don't," Adam insisted.

"You don't think my sister's ugly?" Aileen asked.

"No, of course not," Adam said, not wanting to be mean.

"Then that can only mean one thing," Noelle said.

"You think she's cute!" The three girls giggled in unison.

Aileen started texting someone.

"The little nerd has a crush. Isn't that cute?" Noelle taunted. "Adam has a crush on Marnie!"

"I do not," Adam protested.

"Adam has a crush on Marnie! Adam has a crush on Marnie!" the three girls chanted together.

Adam shook his head and went upstairs. In the kitchen, Zeph and Sapphie were playing with an old sock. Mrs. Hollinger had told Courtney that Sapphie had to stay in the kitchen for the rest of the night, as the girls didn't seem focused enough to care for the small puppy.

Adam played fetch with them, but he did so half-heartedly. The school year hadn't even started yet, and already Adam was being

Corgi Capers: Deceit on Dorset Drive

taunted. Maybe even being a pitcher in Autumn League couldn't help him. Maybe he *was* that much of a nerd. After all, even his parents seemed to side with Courtney most of the time, letting her get away with whatever she wanted.

"Adam," Mrs. Hollinger called down from upstairs. "Mister Ellison sent over that comic book of yours. It's on the kitchen table." She was silent a moment, then added, "I made sure it didn't fall off this time!"

Adam smiled. In the craziness of the burglary, the puppies, the try-outs — and now with his arm sore from pitching all the time, Adam had completely forgotten about the comic. Baseball practice was so intense now that even Patrick had forgotten to ask Adam to return it. As Adam opened the crisp new pages, he realized he hadn't finished reading the story. It had gotten destroyed before he was able to.

He played with the puppies some more. When he took them outside before bed, he went out the front door and all the way around to the back yard, rather than cut through the family room where he'd have to face the three girls again. Then he snuck up to bed early with Patrick's new comic book tucked carefully under his arm.

Corgi Capers: Deceit on Dorset Drive

~ THIRTY-THREE ~
Onward and Upward

"How's your leg, Zeph?" Sapphie asked from her crate that night.

"Sore," he admitted. "But it was worth it. We helped catch the right guy. And now Dad has his computer back."

"Where is Dad? I haven't seen him in a while."

"He's out in his office. He's got a lot of catching up to do, now that his computer is back."

"Zeph? What's a computer?"

Zeph considered a moment. "I'm not really sure." He made a mental note to find out.

"Want to hear something funny?" Sapphie asked while yawning.

"Sure."

"The girls downstairs are going to play a prank on Adam," she said happily.

"What?" Zeph sat straight up.

"Oh, relax, old man. It's a funny trick."

"Adam is my Person," Zeph said. "It's my duty to protect him. What's the trick?"

Sapphie laughed. "Even if I told you, it's not like you could do anything about it. You can't slip out of your crate. You don't know how to open the door like I do. And besides, even if you knew how to do it, you'd probably be too scared to go through with it."

Corgi Capers: Deceit on Dorset Drive

Zeph pondered for a moment. She was probably right. Breaking out of a crate should be saved for only the most dire emergencies. Otherwise, People would become suspicious.

Luckily, the Hollingers had been so confused by the events of the day Mr. Frostburg was arrested that they never questioned how the dogs got loose — they assumed someone forgot to put them inside the kitchen.

"Fine, you're right," Zeph admitted. "But tell me the trick."

"They're going to take Adam's new backpack, the one he just got yesterday, and they're going to draw a little heart on it. And you know what it's going to say inside the heart?"

"No, what?"

"It's going to say *Adam Loves Ms. Wilkerson!*" Sapphie laughed.

"That's not funny, Sapphie. It's a mean trick, and it's something Adam's already upset about. I heard the girls teasing him about it earlier."

"Whatever, you old grump." Sapphie huffed before she rolled over and fell asleep.

Zeph, on the other hand, did not fall asleep. He had to think of something he could do to save Adam from embarrassment. Writing on a backpack wasn't enough of an emergency to warrant sneaking out of a crate, but maybe there was something else he could do.

~ * ~

Corgi Capers: Deceit on Dorset Drive

Upstairs, Adam started reading the comic book from the beginning again. He'd barely made it to the part where Princess Sapphire asked Logan Zephyr to stay on the quicksand planet forever when Zeph started barking and barking.

Adam rushed down to the kitchen. Mr. and Mrs. Hollinger soon followed.

"What's gotten into Zeph?" Mrs. Hollinger asked. It was usually Sapphie — not Zeph — who made noise at bedtime.

"He looks okay," Mr. Hollinger said.

"Maybe his leg hurts," Mrs. Hollinger suggested. "Maybe he needs his medicine."

"Maybe he needs to go outside," Adam said.

They let Zeph out of the crate and let him run downstairs. There, instead of going to the door to go out, he rushed to the girls, who were quietly drawing something on a backpack.

Even Mrs. Hollinger could smell the chemical stink of a permanent marker.

"Girls," she said, coming down the stairs. "What are you doing?"

"Nothing," Courtney lied.

"Is that my new backpack?" Adam asked, looking over at them.

"No," Courtney lied again.

"Is it?" Mrs. Hollinger asked.

"No," Courtney said. Mrs. Hollinger crossed her arms. "Well, maybe."

Corgi Capers: Deceit on Dorset Drive

"Courtney!" Noelle and Aileen protested.

"What are you doing to Adam's backpack?" Mrs. Hollinger asked.

"Nothing."

"Let me see it," Mrs. Hollinger insisted.

"Quick, scribble it out," Aileen said.

"Not so fast!" Mrs. Hollinger grabbed the backpack from them. She read the message they had written inside the heart.

"Girls, I'm disappointed in you. This was Adam's brand-new backpack, and now you've ruined it. It's fine being a giggly teen — or pre-teen — but there's a line you can't cross, and you girls have just crossed it. It's too late to call your parents to pick you up but the sleepover's through. It's lights out right now. Right this minute."

"Let me see it," Adam said.

"Don't worry about it, Adam. I'll buy you a new bag. And Courtney, we'll talk about this in the morning."

"Let me see it," Adam insisted.

Mrs. Hollinger handed him the backpack.

Adam read it: *Adam loves Ms. Wilkerson.*

"Give me the marker," he demanded.

The girls looked at him.

"Give it to me," he repeated.

They did and watched as Adam scratched out the heart and the message in-

Corgi Capers: Deceit on Dorset Drive

side. He was left with an ugly smudge on an otherwise brand-new bag.

"Adam, we'll get you a new one," his mother said again.

"Don't be wasteful. Besides, I'm used to it."

He stormed up to his room and went straight to bed, where he lay awake for hours just staring at the darkened ceiling.

~ * ~

The next morning, Courtney's friends left very early. Courtney was made to eat breakfast with the rest of the family, where she was told she was grounded from her cell phone for the next ten days.

"Ten days! It was just a stupid little prank on a stupid little nerd."

"And that's the attitude we just can't have in this house," Mr. Hollinger said. "Hand over your phone."

"No," she shrieked.

"Hand it over, or we'll cancel your service permanently."

Courtney's eyes teared as she handed over the phone and watched in horror as Mr. Hollinger powered it down. Just as he was doing so, a last-minute text came in but she'd have to wait ten days to see what it said.

"Do you have any idea how unfair you're being? The first week of school starts tomorrow. Everyone's going to have a cell phone. I'll be the only one without one. The only one out of the loop!"

Corgi Capers: Deceit on Dorset Drive

"You mean you'll actually have to focus on your classes?" Mrs. Hollinger asked. "I think it'll be good for you."

"You're all so mean. I hate everyone!" she yelled and stormed out of the kitchen.

Sapphie ran after her. A minute later, her door slammed so hard that a picture hanging in the kitchen rattled.

"Good grief!" Mr. Hollinger said. "We should have been harder on her all along." He turned to Adam. "I sure hope you don't act like that when you become a teenager."

Adam couldn't imagine ever acting like that.

"So what do you want to do on your last day of summer vacation?" Mr. Hollinger asked. "After practice, that is."

Adam shrugged. "After practice, I'd just like to sit somewhere with Zeph and finally finish reading that comic book."

~ * ~

Practice was tiring but satisfying. Adam pitched most of the time, and he was sore when it was over. He was getting better and better at pitching, and Coach Harris wanted to use him in more innings. There were about eight weeks until the regional championships — games would be starting soon — and Coach Harris was getting tougher on the boys.

After he got home, Adam plopped down on his bed with Zeph sitting at his feet. After wearing cleats all day, he felt like he was floating in a cloud. The air coming in from his

Corgi Capers: Deceit on Dorset Drive

open bedroom window was cool and refresh-
ing with just a hint of autumn. He opened the
crisp pages of the comic book and finished
reading.

In the story, Princess Sapphire asked,
then demanded, that Logan Zephyr and his
crew permanently move to the Sapphire Kingdom. Logan at first tried to tiptoe around
Princess Sapphire's question. Logan didn't
want to stay on the planet, but he needed the
princess' help to get his ship back into space.
The more Logan tried to avoid the question,
and the kinder he tried to be, the more vi-
cious the princess seemed. She made him feel
guilty about leaving, and she threatened not
to help him go at all.
Finally, Logan had to stop being so
nice. He had to beat her at her own game. He
threatened to radio a message to earth, re-
vealing the secret kingdom under the quicksand.
"Lots of prospectors will be eager to
come to the secret kingdom. They'll mine for
sapphires, or maybe they'll turn it into an in-
tergalactic amusement park," he told the
princess.
The princess turned pale, then green.
She looked like she might be sick.
"I'd never want that," she said.
Finally, she agreed to release Logan.
She even stocked his ship with food and
helped it break through the swirling quicksand

Corgi Capers: Deceit on Dorset Drive

of the planet's surface.

As the spaceship left the planet's orbit, Logan confessed to his squadron that their radio didn't work under the thick layer of quicksand. He had been bluffing the whole time.

And it had worked!

"So Logan Zephyr got what he wanted," Adam said. "And the princess was taught not to boss him around."

"Adam!" Mrs. Hollinger called. "Courtney! We're going for ice cream! Come on down!"

Adam raced down the stairs with Zeph. Courtney, who hadn't left her room all day even to eat, emerged with a tear-streaked face. She stood next to her brother in the entryway of the house.

"As soon as I get my phone back," Courtney mumbled after her parents had gone outside, "I'm going to spread so many rumors about you. You'll be sorry you got my phone taken away."

Adam's stomach twisted with nerves, and he opened his mouth to plead with his sister. But then he stopped. He remembered Logan Zephyr and the way he had fought back against the princess. Logan Zephyr had been bluffing when he threatened the princess, but it had worked. Maybe it was time for Adam to take a stand, too.

Adam smiled. "I'd be careful what you do to me, Courtney," he said. "Mom and Dad told me if I wanted to, I could get a cell

Corgi Capers: Deceit on Dorset Drive

phone of my own. And maybe I'll have my own rumors to spread."

"Like what?" Courtney asked, an edge of fear in her voice.

"Well, I could take a picture of your dirty clothes all over your room and send it to all of your friends," Adam lied.

He tried to keep a straight face as he watched his sister for a reaction. He knew she liked everyone at school to think she was so neat. Her messy clothes pile was something she wanted to be kept a secret.

"I'm sure everyone would love to see pictures of your underwear!" Adam smirked.

"You wouldn't do that," she whispered.

"I wouldn't be too sure."

Courtney frowned. "Fine," she said after a moment. "I'm sorry I wrote on your stupid backpack. And I'll go easy on you from now on. Just promise you won't send any pictures of my stuff. Okay?"

"Okay." Adam nodded.

It wasn't as big of a victory as Logan Zephyr's, but it was a start. It certainly was a start.

"Come out here, kids," Mr. Hollinger said. "Look how beautiful it is! It's like summer's last hurrah."

The four people and the two puppies looked across the front lawn and into the tree-enshrouded neighborhood. A scattering of fireflies twinkled in the darkening twilight.

Corgi Capers: Deceit on Dorset Drive

They blinked like the stars in the heavens, or sapphire gems shining in a magnificent kingdom.

"You guys want to walk to *Molly's*?" Mr. Hollinger asked.

Adam and Courtney nodded. Molly's was the mom-and-pop ice cream shop a few blocks away that made the best chocolate-coconut milkshakes.

"Let's go," Mr. Hollinger said. "Before it gets too late. After all, this *is* a school night."

Both Adam and Courtney groaned at the thought of early bedtimes from now on.

"Zeph," Sapphie whispered, "what's 'school?'"

Zeph shook his head, indicating that he couldn't talk with People around.

Adam took Zeph's leash, and Courtney took Sapphie's, and the six of them walked in silent amazement at the magnificent summer night, on toward the ice cream shop in the shimmering moonlight and under the sparkling stars, and onward toward their future.

~ END ~

Corgi Capers: Deceit on Dorset Drive

About the Corgis:

Leia and Yoda are sister-and-brother Pembroke Welsh Corgis. The inspiration behind Sapphie and Zeph, they found their Person serendipitously as she drove home from an early movie one morning.

Like Sapphie, Leia is wild and curious and always ready to get into trouble. She spends her days chasing squeaky toys around the kitchen and guarding the container of dog food from her brother.

Yoda, named for the way his huge ears stick into the air, is terrified of most things, including magazines, Leia, and wooden bridges. The corgis are thrilled to be "famous" by serving as inspiration for the stars of this book and by modeling for the cover. They plan to celebrate by eating homemade dog biscuits and chasing a red laser around the kitchen.

About the Corgis' Person:

Author Val Muller was born in Norwalk, Connecticut, where she developed an overactive imagination. She's been writing since she could first hold a pencil and continued doing so through school at Franklin & Marshall College and The College of William and Mary.

She became our person in 2009 when we adopted her. Val didn't realize how much she needed us or how much we would con-

Corgi Capers: Deceit on Dorset Drive

tribute to her writing. Without us, Corgi Capers would never have happened. We will ac-
cept belly rubs in lieu of royalties.

Oh yeah, Val currently teaches English
in Virginia, where she lives with her husband,
our second-favorite person. You can keep
track of her latest writings about us at:

http://mercuryval.wordpress.com
http://CorgiCapers.wordpress.com

Made in the USA
Middletown, DE
01 May 2015